MY JOURNEY TO SAFETY

From South Sudan

PETER ABUI

authorHOUSE®

AuthorHouse™
1663 Liberty Drive
Bloomington, IN 47403
www.authorhouse.com
Phone: 1 (800) 839-8640

Published by AuthorHouse 12/29/2015

ISBN: 978-1-5049-6361-9 (sc)
ISBN: 978-1-5049-6362-6 (e)

Print information available on the last page.

CONTENTS

AUTHOR'S ACKNOWLEDGMENTS

"Where are you from?" "Do you like it here?" "Will you go back there (to S. Sudan)?" "What made you come to America?" These are all questions that I have been asked by anyone that I have met since my relocation to America. In this story, I will be able to answer all of these questions and in more depth then I have been able to do in person. The story that you are about to read is the story of my life. In my personal experiences, these are my experiences and may not be the same as another Sudanese—lost boys. It is my hope that by telling my story, it will bring me some much needed closure. I have struggled within myself to come to terms with some of the things that I have gone through. I can assure you that it was much harder to live. Writing them down has helped me work through these difficult times of my life. I must warn you that the retelling of my journey may be graphic and hard to read. It may also be difficult to understand due to some of the language that I use. Some of the things such as names of places, games, or names of people are in my native language, Dinka. Other times I may use my language because I don't know the English word for it. "Do not be frustrated with these non-English words you might come across through your reading. Just try to get the message I'm trying to say to you and to the world."

I have asked for help from some of my family members back in S. Sudan in order to fill in some of the holes of my memory. Some of the things that happened in the beginning are harder for me to remember because I was so young. My brothers and even my mother have been able to help me with this part.

The war that forced me out of my home in South Sudan to other countries, the desert that I crossed to Ethiopia in 1988 and To Kenya in 1992, and the time when I came to the United Stated of America are the moments I remember. "For me to find a word Will describes all these places is obvious." Color-coding is the best word I can think of to label all these places' base on the fact events that have had happened on these days. In my mind, I picked out a color for each of these places to symbolize my emotional feeling. I decided to put more information and details into this book so people can understand and know more about my past life. There are even some reflections, which you can find at the end of the book.

The red color represents the danger of war that I escaped from South Sudan to neighboring countries. I pick this red color to describe the pain that this war had caused me.

The tan color reminds me of the long desert that I crossed on a bar foot without water or food to Ethiopia in 1988. It was very a hard moment; every bad thing you can think of, happened to me on my way to Ethiopia camp and to other refugee camps I had been to.

The green color represents the time when I was arriving to the United States of America and the time when I was still in Kalthok, South Sudan before the war broke out. I picked this color green as a sign of freedom and happiness. This color reminds me of those good old days I spent with my family and friends back home in Kalthok, south Sudan. "Life was good back then and I'm not forgetting that moment even though I didn't enjoy it for so long." Though I didn't really remember any of the good the times due to childhood lack of memories, I'm very sure those days were very fantastic.

SPECIAL THANKS

I would like to take this opportunity to give thanks to the government of the United States of America for the warm welcome to the country. And to the State of Vermont, for their hospitality and support. Many thanks go to the Vermont Refugee Resettlement Program for setting me up with my very first apartment, job, and any other thing that I needed to start my new life here in Vermont, such as setting up doctor appointments and showing me how to buy my own food.

Mother Rachel Hutchins, for enrolling me in an ESL (English as some second languages) class and helping me open my very own bank account. Thanks to George and Dorothy Cross for becoming my sponsor family. For teaching me how to drive and helping me finding my first car. For making me feel apart of their family. Joseph and Bonnie Maietta and their children; Tina, Roxanne, and Todd for always including me in their family events. For all the love, hugs, kisses & gifts that I received every thanksgivings and Christmas. To Momma Jean, for quick responses to my calls whenever I needed a ride or to go shopping before I got my license. For any and all legal advice. Helping me with immigration paperwork and statuses. To all my teachers including Karen Archer, for believing in me and helping me see my potential. Lauren Couillard for helping me files my income taxes every year. For always encouraging me to further my education and establish my career goals. To Mrs. Paw Landry for helping me contact my car insurance when I had car accident and nobody I know was around to talk to.

Lastly some specials thank you to my wonderful wife, Patricia Abui. For always being supportive and understanding. She continues to encourage me in every way. For always being there for me when I need her the most and for helping me put together this story of my journey in a way that makes sense.

CHAPTER 1

My life before the war In Kalthok, South Sudan

My name is Majuch Abui Gongich (Peter) from Kalthok South Sudan. This is the name my parents decided to call me after my grandfather. I later became known as Peter later in life, which I will explain a little bit later. I am the second child born of the Abui family. I have three brothers including me. I do not have any sisters. My father Abui had three siblings, Dokok, Abahor, and Nyakuei. They both have children of their own. He was not a chief of the clan but he was well known for his sense of humor. I guess he was a funny man. He made everybody laugh. At least that is what people have told me about him. I never talked to him face to face or sat on his lap for that matter. He died before I was born. I learn about him from my older brother Ring and my mother. I am told that my biological father; Abahor Mayom, my mother first husband's brother, might have held me or I sat on his lap when I was little but other than that I do not have any thing to remember about him either. I was separated from my family before I got to know him more and before I did any heavy outside work with him when I was still there.

Abui had two wives, Nyadit Jok and my mother Apuot Nyadier. My mother had Ring with her first husband Abui; followed by me, my brother Maluch, and lastly my brother Agau, by my biological father, Abahor, my mother's second husband brother. My brother Ring has two wives and has four children. Also, my brother Maluch got married to Regina Ponie Kenny from Mundari tribe and they had four children together as well. Agau got married after Maluch and he had one child as of right now. I myself got married to a beautiful American woman, Patricia Abui, and we have three children together; Maluchy, which I named him after my brother, Maluch; Methderow, and Majuch.

My family didn't have many cattle except goats and sheep, which I used to look after them at the time in Kalthok, South Sudan. However, we lost all of them in 1988 when my village was attack by the Arab north regime and everything was burned down.

The family of my mother side is big. My grandfather Nyandier had six children. My mother is the third child born of the Nyandier family. I never have a chance to see both of my grandparents except my grandmother Amath Kot on my mother side. The rest of my grandparents died before

1

I was born. I used to go and staying with my grandmother Amath Kot in her house when I was little. She was still a live when I left home in 1988. I met all of my aunts and uncles at the time of my present.

The day that I was born is unknown to me. My mother gave birth in the hut that my father Abahor built, in the small village called Kalthok. I don't know the day or month that this took place, not even the year! My mother, Deborah Apout, may know the season I was born, but I doubt she knows the year or exact day of my birth. The Dinka people have their own way of keeping tract of time. The most important thing to the Dinka is not the day or week but the season. Dinka people are farmers and cattle herders. They start counting each day of the month when they see a full moon. This is the beginning of the month for them. They know when to cultivate when it begins to rain. The cattle herders know that this is the time to move the cattle so they do not ruin the crops. When the rain stops the people will harvest their crops and then the cattle will return to the village. The returning of the cattle after harvest is calling Abuong.

My culture is what I remember the most during all the years of my residing in refugee camps outside of South Sudan. I do not remember many of the good and bad things I did when I was still back home in Kalthok. Dinka culture was the only thing I was born into and lived around it for six years in Kalthok. I saw the culture itself, and I used to listen to it all the time; that mean I saw all the culture activities that people do in daily life such as dancing, traditional songs, and stories.

Therefore, every time I want to tell my life story then culture always comes in my memory.

My people of Kalthok, South Sudan is very proud people. We have many traditions that we hold dearly, family being one of the most important. One of the traditions that I love most is the way we take care of our own. For example, if a man dies leaving behind a wife or wives, than the brother of the man or a close relative will take over the duties of his family including marrying the wife and raising the children, he may have had. This is to ensure that your name lives on in the clan. I am a good example of this particular tradition. My mother was married to a man named Abui Majuch Gongwich. While they were married, my mother had a son, my oldest brother, Ring. Abui passed away before my mother had any more children. The elders agreed that Abahor Mayoum, a brother to Abui, would marry my mother and take over as her husband to carry on Abui's name. My mother than went on and had 3 more sons, I included. So technically my brother Agau, Maluch, and I were inheritance children to Abui family.

Because Abui's first wife did not have any boys, in Dinka culture it is expect of his first son to marry a woman on behalf of Nyandit, Abui's first wife. The children that he has with this wife are to be name after Abui as if her son would do. This is to ensure that her family name will continue. This responsibility fell upon my oldest brother, Ring. The only son that Abui had with my mother before he passed a way. My mother was Abui's second wife and Nyadit Jok was his first wife. When a man marries a woman because her first husband died. It is expected of that man to honor the life of the first husband by naming any children he has with the woman, after the dead husband. The elders of the dead man will choose a suitable relative to marry the widow, but the widow does have some to say. She is allowed to reject the man they chose and offer an alternative, as long it is within the clan. Ultimately, the elders get the final approval though.

Back home in Kalthok, South Sudan, I used to look after my uncle Doko's sheep and goats together with our sheep and goats as well. One day, one of the sheep had gone missing for a whole week. Turns out the sheep took off with our neighbor Mr. Nyitong's herd of sheep. I got in trouble that day by my dad for let the sheep disappeared. My father Abahor was not happy with me at all. He thought I was careless and not being a responsible person. I was so upset for being yelled at for just one missing sheep. However, it was a big deal to my dad because these livestock's were our income resources. We rely on them for food to survive. I realized it was my fault for the sheep disappearing. The Following week Mr. Nyitong came to our house with good news about the lost sheep. "I had one of your sheep with my sheep," said Mr. Nyitong. I was standing a couple feet away from my dad and Mr. Nyiton when they were talking, I pretended I was not listening to their conversation. Because little kids aren't allowed to listening to adults' conversation, it is Dinka culture. From that day, I became more careful looking after our sheep, goats, and none of them had gone missing ever again.

I missed those quiet, peaceful, breezy nights with bright moonlight and stars in the blue sky. I used to play all kinds of games such as Aleuth, Agach, Wuntek, Adiir, and Anyok in empty field of the peanut at evening hours with my friends.

We used to tell ourselves stories every night when getting together to play. These games were very important to young children in a village of Kalthok, Southern Sudan. There weren't other activities that entertain people such as football game, baseball, basketball, and soccer game just like here in America except to play these traditional games once the sun goes down or any time in a day. I didn't take anything especial with me for the memory of my home land when I left South Sudan. The only thing that I had with me all these years of my traveling around the world looking for safety place was these traditions' culture stories and games.

These stories and games weren't in the book to read them in word but only in my memory. Not all the games and stories I heard when I was still at home, I remembered, only the especial ones with a meaningful message as the one below:

The game of Aleuth is similar to the game of tag. One person stands at one end of the field, while the rest of the group stands on the other end of the field. The game leader asks questions and the group have to answer it.

"Aleuth, shout the game leader."
Mochol, the groups respond.

What is in a jar? Asked the game leader.
There is milk in a jar, the groups answered.
Whose milk? Asked the game leader.
Diang's milk, the group Answered.
Where did he go? Asked the game leader
He went to the restroom, the group answered.
What for? Asked the game leader.
Constipation! The group answered.
Why do not you pull it out? Asked the game leader.

Pull it out! Our hands will get stain, the groups answered.
Then the groups run toward the other end of the field dodging the game leader while the game leader tried to touch them and if he does touch you then you are out of the game. The last remaining person won the game.

Another game is Agach. Young men love it a lot because it all about impressing girls. The purpose of the game is to show your manhood to girls that you are a good singer. All boys have to sit on one side and girls on one side. One girl at a time has to get up and chose one man of her interests, and then the chosen one has to come up with the best song of his favor color of any bull to empress the girl. If the boy fails to sing, the girls have to sing vulture song to disappoint that boy for not singing his song. However, if he sung his good song, then, the girls can sing especial song for him and a girl dance together with a boy.

The song goes like this: the cloth of Tali is so bright.
The cloth of Rumbek is so bright.
The cloth is so shinny so white like a clear moon in the sky.
Game of Wuntek
People site on line with their legs stretches out then one a person has to start counting and singing a song of Wuntek at the same time while counting people legs.

Wuntek wuntek aaaaa gramma Nyejuai is inside the house waiting for her milk to arrive from cattle camp perch in shell.

Girls of cattle camp of whom?

Girls of cattle camp of Nyejuai will divide milk between the tilling and Malakak Oh yeah.
Nyejuai's sister is inside the house oh yeah.

If the song end while the game leader's hand land on either your left or right leg then you have to hide that leg by sitting on it.

If you lose all your legs, then you lost the game and the last person left won the game.

Game of Adiir! I compared this game of Adiir with American Hockey game because it is just like hockey except no ice ring for Adiir but only on big open field. The players used the same Adiir stick as hockey stick, long and it is made out of wood.

They Adiir itself is cut out of wood too, is round exactly just like the size of a puck but a little bit heavy. Young men of Dinka love Adiir game so much; they play it only in morning when the sun is not too hot. People divided themselves into two groups' then one group on one side of the field-standing couple of inches away from a person next to you. The other group has to do the same procedures on the other end of the field. Adiir is a game without rules, no couch or referee; this game is very dangerous. Not a chance a kid can go near where people play this game because of the way they hit it and fly, so scary! The players do not even wear protected gear and that's what make it so dangerous. It is up to each player to make sure the puck do not hit him. One side serves the game by hitting harder as they could and the other will hit it back without stopping it. The aim of the game is not to let the Adiir past you otherwise it is a score goal.

This game of Anyok (baobab) also is a dangerous one because of the sharp object used to play it. Anyok is the type of tree that produces fruits just like a baobab tree and it is none eatable. It has a long and strong stalk hanging down from its attaching point in the tree with the fruits at the end of stem. The only place I used to see this tree was a long the river Guar in kalthok, Belook area. They young men cut the Anyok down from its attaching point. One person could take control of Anyok by standing in center of field and spin the Anyok around him while staying foot. One brave man had to go where the person spinning Anyok standing and begin to throw his stick at the Anyok however, whether he hits it or not, the Anyok person will pursue him back to where everybody is standing tried to strike him. Meanwhile, the groups of other young men waited to strike Anyok with sharp end stick the game players always tried to aim theirs sharp stick at the Anyok. You do not strike at a person though just only the Anyok itself. This game no loser or winner but just to have funned and proving yourself that you are the man and ran fast.

I heard very much most of the Dinka culture stories that had been told by parents and young adults when I was still in Kalthok Village before I left home. My mother and my big brother Ring with his friends used to tell me stories during the bedtime, I listen until I fell asleep.

The story of the wisdom woman Korjok, Frog and Rabbit, and the story of the lost man from another world was the one that kept my enthusiasm going! These stories were my invisible imaginary therapy councillors. "They slow down my mind when I was in sorrow thinking mood!"

The story of the lost man and the story of the wisdom woman both got different points of view. "The story of the lost man is bout struggling and hope." "The story of the wisdom woman Korjok is all about not losing hope on somebody even though you know they are not always there for you.

It's also about the family stick together no mater what." These two stories kept my motivation a life because when I have nightmares I think of this story of the lost man from another world by imagining it as I follow along just like as either my mother or my brother Ring is telling it to me out loud and that make I fell back to sleep. One of my brother's friends used to tell me this story of the lost man from another world every time when he comes to my house for sleep over which make it even more to stuck in my head.

A man from another world who got lost and did n't know where he was; because he went to another village to look for his lost cow. One day he came to a town where a magician is in charge of telling the fairy tale. The lost man told the magic man his problem and he wish to go back home where he belong. I will see what I can do, said the magic man. The magic man brought out two goats, one black and the other one white. The magic man put blindfold on the lost man and told him to find a white goat among the two. If you touch the white goat then you will go back home, but if you slab the back of the black goat thus, you will end up in the under world, said the magic man.

The lost man did the test as the magic man told him to do. After he was blindfold, he walked toward the goats and tried to slab the back of a white goat, but instead he touched the black goat, which took him to the under world.

The under world was rule by a king and a queen and they had a beautiful princess.

"The kingdom was facing some problem regardless of danger and unsafe living condition." There is a lake that surrounding the city and inside that lake was a big, big snake with twelve heads. This snake eats nothing else but human being!, Therefore, the people of that city take turn contributing food for the snake which mean each family has to give one child to a snake every year. That year of the lost man from another world his appearing was the king's turn to gift something to a snake. The king had only one child, his princess however, the king has no choice but to let his daughter goes in order to save his kingdom and the people.

Following morning, the king took his daughter to the shore where the snake always waited for his meal. The guards made princess stand on the shore couple of inches away from the water lake. At noontime, the snake started to approach a girl on the shore then the lost man arrived to the shore where the girl is standing.

What are you doing here? You are not supposed to be here! Asked the princess. I do not know! I do not really know where am I right now? Said the lost man from another world.

What about you? What are you doing here on lake alone? Asked the lost man.

"I'm supposed to be Snake's meal for the day" the princess replies.

What for? Asked the lost man.

As a gift to a snake to save my kingdom and my people, the princess said.

That is not going to happen, said the lost man.

Just go home to your mother and father, said the lost man.

What are you going to do? You cannot kill this monster snake by yourself, said the princess.

Do not you worry just go home, I will try my best to protect myself, said the lost man.

The princess went home to her parents.

What are you doing back here princess? Asked the king and queen.

Some man let me come home, the princess replies.

Some man! But who, who's strong enough to defeat that snake? Asked the king.

Go! Back, go! Back princess, the king repeated.

No! I cannot father, the man already made his mind to stay there instead of me, said the princess.

As the time goes by the Snake got hungry so he moved closer where the man was standing and raises his one head out and tried to swallow the man. Then the lost man from another world took his sword out and cut the snake's one head off and another head, one after another head until the snake is dead.

The lost man went to the city after the snake was dead.

From that movement, the king wanted to meet the man who saves his daughter's life from that monster Snake to be his son's in-law. The king called the big meeting in the city to announce his decision about his daughter. Therefore, everyone in the city to come to the meeting.

Whoever safe my daughter from that monster snake! If you are here show yourself, said the king.

Every man tried to claim the price. The king has no idea how the lost man looks like but, the princess dose. So the men all lines up in single filed and then the king's daughter has to identify the man who saves her from a snake. When the lost man arrived to the meeting, he decided not to joint in, he waited until the line is gone then he approaches the princess. The princess recognizes the man right away. She pulled the man close and hugged him.

You are a life, Said the princess.
Yes I am a life; I kill the snake so your kingdom is safe now, Said the lost man.

I cannot belief you did it, Said the princess.

The lost man from another world marriage to the king's daughter and the both live Together happily forever and ever.

The lost man decided not to struggle any more of finding the way back home. He started to build his new life there and "hope" that, in one day he would find the way home.

My story is like the story of the lost man from another world. Except I wasn't ends up in Ethiopia because I was lost but because I was running away from war that drop me out of my home. I had been into three different places and I was anxious to go back home. All the years of my traveling, I was hoping that, one day I will be able to reunited with my family again.

I think of this story of Korjodit every time when I am home sick. Korjokdit was a wisdom woman with ten children of her own. She had five girls and five boys.

After they all grown up they get marriage and move out with their families.

Korjokdit was live alone at home. One night a lion came to her house and demanded her to give up her all belonging or the lion will kill her. However, she did not have any possessive such as sheep or goat that the lion would want. She said to a lion, please before you take my life can I say goodbye to my children who knows may be one of them will provide what you needed. The lion agreed to let Korjokdit go and say goodbye to her children. It was raining that night so it was cold. The lion warned Korjokdit to make goodbye business quick and short before daylight. Thank you, said Korjokdit to a lion. Then the both head the road to her firstborn son. When she got to the house, she knocked the door and said my son's family, open the door for your mother. Then her son asked, Who are you?

Korjokdit answered him back, I am your mother Korjokdit.

Her son asked again, what are you doing here in middle of the night mother Korjokdit?

Korjokdit answered, I am in big trouble, the lion wanted to kill me so I come here if you could owe me some goat or sheep to take care of this burden.

Her son replied, I do not have a sheep or goat mother to give you mother so Mr. Lion go ahead and takes her for an appetizer.

She went to a second born daughter's house. She stated the same message to her second born daughter just exactly like the way she said it to her first son.

However, the second born daughter provides nothing to her mother Korjokdit as well. Korjokdit then went to her third born son's house and to fourth; fifth, sixth, seventh, eight, and nine but they all said the same thing to their mother. None of her nine children open the door for theirs mother Korjokdit. She finally went to her last born son's home away in different town. When she reached there, she knocked on a door and said she, my son's family open the door for your mother.

Her son asked, who are you? Korjokdit answered, I am your mother Korjokdit. Her son asked again, what are you doing here in middle of the night mother Korjokdit?

Korjokdit answered, I am here because I am in a big trouble, the lion wanted to kill me so I come here if you could owe me some goat or sheep to take care of this burden.

Her son replied, I do not have any goat or sheep mother to owe you.

Her son walked toward the door and he opens the door. He said to a lion, you look cold just come in and warm up before you head the road. The lion agreed to come in and warm up a little bit.

Korjokdit her last-born son got a plan. He put a round metal in a fire while a lion was not looking and let it burn until its turn brownish. He took it out and said to Mr. Lion, it is my pleasure to have you into my home so here is the gift to you as my an opportunity to welcome you to my house. Open your mouth and I will put this nice roasting fat meat of a goat into your mouth. The lion was so happy for the gift therefore, he opens his mouth wide and then Korjokdit's last born son drops that burning metal into lion's throat and kill a lion. Now her last son who really cares about his mother had broken Korjokdit's burden.

My uncle Nhial Cholkeny reminded me about this story of a Frog and a Rabbit at the time of my visited to South Sudan in 2009 for the first time in 21 years. He told this story when we were in meeting on Sunday afternoon in Juba, South Sudan.

The reason he told the story was to work together as one and care of one another even though you do not have power to do it. It was his turn to talk, he started talking and he just started telling the story. The kingdom was rule by a king Frog and he had a princess daughter. One of the Frogmen was in love with the princess and wanted to marriages her. However, a Rabbit wanted to marriage king Frog's daughter as well. The princess was so confuse whom to choose between a Frog and a Rabbit. Therefore, she went to her father and told him the situation so her father could make suggestion of what to do. The king Frog did not have another opinion but for the two men to do a marathon race. He did not want to disappoint his daughter by choosing the man of his interest. Princess loves both Frog and Rabbit, however she was really confused. After talking to her Father and then her father came up with the idea of marathon race, the princess agreed with the idea.

The marathon was schedule for next morning. That night the Frog calls the meeting to discuss the possibility of winning because, he knew he is not a fast runner. They came up with one solution not to let only the boyfriend of the king Frog's daughter princess race with Rabbit alone. However, from the starting point to the finish line, one frog put in place every couple of feet apart from one another. When the race started, Rabbit was so excited he knew is going to win the race and marriage the girl. However, he did not know Frog's plan. The two men began the race; Rabbit was far a head of Rabbit already. Couple of feet a head the other Frog jumps out in front of Rabbit and a Rabbit past him again. The other Frog did the same by jumping out in front of a Rabbit hopping as past as he could and a Rabbit past him again. Then the other one and the next one at the finish line jump out to the finish line. Rabbit did not know what he did wrong to make him lose. Now the Frog claims the victory to marriage princess. Even though Frog cheated, they did it for the care and teamwork.

Giving birth in South Sudan is a lot different than here in the U.S. For example, women in South Sudan do not normally go to the hospital to give birth. The women delivery their babies at home with the help of midwife, mother, and other specialists female members of the community. Men are not allowed anywhere near a woman who is in labor. In fact, the men either will stay just outside the hut or will go visit a neighbor. Giving birth is a woman job and the men stay away.

When the woman and child have been clean up, the father, will then be introduce to his new child, usually 1 or 2 days after birth. Within each village, there is usually at least one midwife, but if there is not then there is in a neighboring village close by. Women do not have the option of an epridural or any type of painkiller. They must give birth naturally. It is amazing how the Dinka mothers take care of theirs babies. In my village of Kalthok, South Sudan, there are no any kinds of baby cleaning tools such as booger sucker, diapers, and baby wipe that available for mother to use in time of need. When a baby is sick with cold or pink eye then a mother has to used a piece of clothes with warm water to clean the baby's face.

Although, not all the time warm water and piece of clothes available, therefore, a mother has to do everything, she could to keep her baby clean.

If a woman experiences a miscarriage then someone might send for a magic man.

A magic man is what you might call a witch doctor or shaman.

I remember a time when I was young; maybe five years old, I was with my mother inside her hut. There was blood all over the ground, flies filled the air and my mother was in a lot of pain. I didn't know it at the time but she was experiencing a miscarriage. I was very scared, I wasn't sure my mother would live. She was sitting in the middle of the hut leaning against the large pole that helped hold the roof up. I felt so helpless, I just sat next to her, holding her hand and crying. It was my aunty, Nyanpiu, who tried to explain it to me, but I just did not understand. I was too young. We were all alone, my mother and I, my brothers were at the cattle camp, and my father was out fishing and hunting for food. He would be gone for a week. My Aunty sent for the magic man, and my mother and I just waited for him to arrive. Mr. Abal Nhial was the name of the magic man. When he arrived at our home, he came in, and without saying a word, he grabbed a bowl of water and four pieces of grass stems. My mother was in so much pain, she said nothing. I was afraid she would die. Mr. Abal Nhial then dipped the grass stems into the water and sprinkled it on my mothers' forehead while saying some magic words.

To this day, I still don't know what it is he was saying. I just watched him conduct his magic. When he left, my mother and I remained in the very same spot. My Aunty came to help clean my mother and to feed her. She had to travel 2 hours from her home to be with us. I was too young to boil even water for my mother.

We don't always rely on the magic of a magic man. Often times we use local medicine plants that are known to help with certain illnesses. It is common to use the roots and seeds from the Riath tree to help with stomach pains, headaches and diarrhea. I remember my mother using this on me when I was a child. She would take the root or seeds, boil them in water, and then make me drink the liquid after it has cooled. Within a few hours, I would be feeling much better.

Every single time if you had Malaria or Yellow fever than Malkaak would be use.

Malkaak is a fruit much like an orange. There is nothing you have to do to prepare this, you just peel it and eat it just like an orange. If you have an open wound such as a cut, we would use the fat that we get from a cow and just apply it to the wound. This keeps it moist and clean. It also helps keep infection away. With burns, you would use the fat from a hippo. Now I am not saying that we would go kill a hippo or cow every time we needed its fat, you would instead purchase it from a merchant. Cow urine is often used to clean burns or cuts. Dinka people use cow urine for many things not just as an antiseptic, it can be use to wash your face, to dye your hair, to clean your containers that you use when milking the cows. The cow plays many important roles to the Dinka people. It is often used as a form of money. To have many cows is the same as having a lot of money. Before the war broke out, the biggest problems among the Dinka people were cattle raids, but even these were few. Dinka people only eat their cattle on special occasions, because you think of it more as a means of money and wealth. There is a certain time when all you eat is cow meat. This time is call Dueel. It is a time when a group of young men and young women come together to celebrate. It is a lot like a way of passage. The Aliab Dinka people love Dueel

11

so much. Some time they do it every two years. The all idea of Dueel is just to eat a lot of cow meat and gain weight. Each person or set of brothers must contribute one bull. All of the bulls that are contributed slaughtered and consumed by the Achilips, which is the name of the group of young adults attending the Dueel. For the boys participating in the Dueel, it is one way of going from being a child to being an adult. By killing your first cow, you are considering a man and no longer a child.

You are then given the nickname of the color cow that you killed. During the time of Dueel celebration, everyone tried to created songs base on Dueel operation. I remember one of the Dueel songs sung by one of the Achilips. I used to sing this song all the time when I was still in Kalthok, south Sudan. "The noisy sound of fry meat is what I want to hear, Abuk mother don't let the boiling meat burn you. I am the man with no curiosity of boiling meat. I just want to drink oil from the cow's fat."

The Rainy season is the most difficult season because by that time, you are low on food and what seeds that remain are the ones that you must plant in order to grow more food. No one ever touched these seeds even though you are dying of hunger. For as far back as one can remember my people have always planted our seeds by hand. We all go to the field, get on our hands and knees, and rake the ground using a hand tool called a hoe. Then you sprinkle the seeds. We don't have to worry about watering the seeds because the rain will do that for us. My mother has her own method to planting crops. Every year she plants certain seeds first such as sweet potato, sweet pumpkin, okra, green beans and groundnuts because they tend to grow faster and because we usually need food by this time. Then she would plant the Sorghum, cassava, and mallets. My mother would plant these seeds at last because they take longest time to grow. The plants will grow relatively quick and healthy as long as the rainy season is steady. If it is, a short season then the plants might dry up before they are ready to be picking. Some times if the rainy a season have not begun yet and you think that it should have by now, some people will call upon a magic man to pray to his gods for rain. There are different types of magic men. If you wanted rain, you would seek one magic man but if you were sick, you might seek a different magic man. Each Magic man has his own area of expertise. I can remember a few times when members of my village called upon a magic man for help bringing the rain.

There was one type of crop called purjula that my father Abahor used to plant separate from other crops so we could identify them easily. This type of plant would grow better when it is separate from other crops for some reasons and I do not know why. In old days, my parents love growing their own food. Back then, cultivation is the only career that village people love to do for the sake of better living.

In time of hardship when food is shortage, my parents always hope for good smiling latter on when harvesting time comes. I learn that ownership requires responsibilities and management. It is a freedom to do what you wish to accomplish in life. My parents did not have other income resources of food but to cultivated their own food. My mother's piece of advice was that, she always told me to accept no failure or any weakness when I have hard time doing something or when I'm in a bad situation, not to stop but to keep going. She told me to find my own stuffs with my own sweat and not to steal or take anything for granted but to work for it. Out of all other pieces of advice she had been told me in my home village of Kalthok, this is the only one that stuck in my head and it kept me alive all these years until then.

My parents used to do this kind of job for living: "Farming" even today's date they are still trying to practice it, even though the fear of foes avoided them from cultivating food for such a long period of time.

When I was with my family before everything fell apart; in time of hardship, I used to wake up every morning and went to play for the day. I was little and did not know what was going on. I always come home so hungry after long day playing with my friends. When I came home, I just wanted to eat something. However, I knew when I left home nothing was cooking. Since there was no refrigerator or pantry to go straight to and look for food, then my only option was to look for smoke or a sign of positive attitude on my mother's face. Perhaps, I could just stick my foot in ash where mother cooks all the time to test if it is hot or cold.

However, if it is hot then there is food being prepared and cold ash mean nothing. Seeing a smile on mother face and she would call me with my nickname,

Mayiech (belly man) that is the sign of the possibility of food available. My mother told me that when I was a baby I would eat a lot. I was even a little chunky, she said. She tells me that I used to beat up the other children. She would call me "Aced Acheng ke diak" which roughly translated means to eat three turtle shells full of food. She told me that if my plate was not full I would just cry for more.

Therefore, to make me happy she would give me 3 turtle shells of food even if there was not a lot in them or just spread out the food in one plate to look big. It would make me happy just to have three shells of food!

I missed those days when my mother Apuot used to tells me jokes all the time. I think she was just tried to me laughs and be happy. I was little so I belief everything she said to me was true. She used to tell me not to laugh when a bay releasing intestinal gust, the bees would be stung you if you laugh, she said. She also, told me not to ever hit any of my brothers with a broom and if I do, that person will pee his bed. I was very sure I never experience all this curiosity. I tried very hard not to laugh when a baby release gust but most of the time it is just impossible not to laugh. Bees never stung me though. I tried to hit my brother Maluch with a broom couple of times but I do not think he did urinate on his bed may be after I was separated with them that he did pee his bed.

It is always my father Abahor's job to make sure there is food on a table for us. He has to go hunt, fishing, and cultivate to feed the family. According to Dinka, culture boys always do the outside heavy works with fathers like cutting down the big trees for firewood and look after cows, and goats. This is how a boy learns to be coming a responsible person so he could take care of his own family later on in life.

Technically, according to my culture, bad boys are the one always-got sends to school because parents belief that school is a place where this bad boy could learn some respect. Parents did not know the important of education back then. Only Dinka people belief that school is for bad and lazy children. The only thing they believe as important was cattle so they a good child always got sent to the cattle camp to look after cows and learn how to take care of cattle. A good boy stays home some time with mother or father to help around the house if there are no cows to look after them in cattle's camp. Also, cattle camp always can change disobedient children's behaviors. That's because of the heavy work they have to do such as cleaning up cow dung and spread them out on open field to dry then put them on fire to burn into ash. A boy has to put every cow on a leash and on post where the cow always stays. Also, it's very important for the boy to know all the leashes to every cow. He/she has to put the leaches in order exactly without missing them up otherwise he/she is in trouble by his/her big brother or father for the miss placement of the leashes. It is very important to know where each leash goes because they are in sizes and length. More important, he/she has to make sure not to turn the knob of the loop of the leash on a left side when place it on a post, always on right. I do not know why they do that. But that is the theory the Dinka cattle keepers believe in. When the cattle camp moves to new area, it is boy's duty to carry all the posts for the cows to be leash down later on when stop. They have to carry the posts to the new cattle camp every time of relocation because it is very hard to make the new post for every cow. It is a boy's responsibility to fetch for firewood for the little calves and also, it is boy's responsibility to look after little calves and not to let them gets lost.

The new kid in a cattle camp always gets harassment from friends and elders because he does n't know anything about the life in cattle camp. First day of cattle camp is like first day at work not knowing what to do if you are not familiar with the job. People harass you calling you home boy (azeek bai). What is weird about cattle camp is that when someone sees you talking to one of your relatives in a disrespectful way he would beat you up even though that person is not related to you. Somebody else from the other side will call you to come to him so he could help you. However, he is lying he would start beating up you too as well when you come to him as like he said. I was wondering why someone who does not even know me wants to beat me up for something he does not know about.

The other person will do the same thing, he called you over to help you but instead he started beating you. Therefore, the best thing to do is just to run to the other directions. A boy who had been in cattle camp for too long will know all the concept of calling over for help as deceiving.

Also, cattle's camp is where the bullying exists. You have to be strong to depend yourself and set up your boundaries otherwise, your friends and your age mates will make your life miserable.

My parent belief that both girls and boys are very important to the society so they are raises and taught by parents to be strong, responsible, and an obedient person. The reason is for them to carry on a family legacy a long the line. In cattle camp or at home, the girl is responsible for the household. She helps mother out with cooking, cleaning, fetch water, and collecting firewood for cooking. In addition, in cattle camp, girls' work is to make food for his brothers and father if they both are at the cattle camp. A girl can help the boy out by milking the cows if there are many cows to be milk otherwise a boy can do the milking business.

In cattle, camp women don't have other work to do except to make butter and look after the children. Making butter is the only thing girls love to do in a free time.

I used to watch girls doing Ghom (the process of butter making) in Buur camp. It is very amazing how women practice this kind of method of making butter out of cow fresh milk. Here in America they used machines to make cheese and butter out of dairy products. But in Aliab area in southern Sudan, women make butter out of a dairy fresh product by using a pumpkin jar. A Girl had to take the pumpkin and remove all the seeds out of it then place it in water for a couple of days so the chunk inside pumpkin to clear off. After that process, the girl takes out pumpkin out of water and put it in Sun to dry and then they crave the plug for the pumpkin out of wood. The girls can even decorate the pumpkin jar by putting black lines across the pumpkin jar using the hot knife tip.

A group of girls may be five to ten would sit in a circle under a tree in which is they call Bur in Dinka during the day light. They shook or banged a pumpkin jar that contains with fresh milk against their lap while singing songs at the same time, the sound of a pumpkin jar and singing making very good music in my ear. At the time of moving to a new cattle camp, it is girl's responsibility to carried all cooking materials and other possessions that she used in daily bases.

Harvesting was always a time for joy because food is available and everyone is happy. There are always all kinds of parties going on in the area; children had fun playing in the fields around the villages. It is important though at the time of the harvest to keep a certain amount of seeds for next years planting. This is crucial because if you eat them all than you will have nothing to plant in coming cultivation time unless you have money to buy new seeds. Having extra money to buy new seeds is very rare. Many people rely on their crops as their only source of income. Some of this money will go toward buy more seeds but you always want to save some from your last harvest so you don't have to use all of your money buying new seeds. My mother always makes sure that she saves some of her seeds. Those few seeds will make it to the next cultivation no matter if you are starving.

I remembered when my mother used to wake up my older brother Ring Abui every morning to watch over our Sorghum and millet garden so the Dove, pigeon, pheasants, quails, and Native sparrows do not destroy them. Ring, my big brother used to take me with him to guard our garden from birds. He taught me how to roast sorghum in hot ash of fire. He also taught me how to identify a certain type of sorghum stem that contains sweet juice in them just by looking at the leaves.

He told me that you could tell if a midrib of the sorghum's leaves is dark gray then that mean it is good to drink juice out of it. You peal the outer party of sorghum and the inside part is the one with juice, you chew it and that's how you got juice out of Sorghum stems. My mother Apout used to cut fish or meat with the outer part of the sorghum stem because it is very sharp.

Sometime my mother plant sesame together with rest of crops in one garden or she could plant sesame separate from other crops so she could find them very easy all in one spot when she needs them. There was no other way to get sesame seeds out of its shell except this type of traditional method called Chirit in Dinka.

My mother, Apuot used to build a slop stage rack out of thicker stick row by row for sesame to be lay on to dry. This is calling Chirit in Dinka. She cuts the sesame down from the garden and ties them up in small bundles then straps them on the stage rack. Underneath the rack was the nice, smooth clean plaster floor. My mother used sand to plastering the floor in order to separate sand out from sesame; there is no cement to smooth up this particular area for sesame but only the muddy sand. When the sesame dried, my mother just took a bat and beat the rack and the seeds fell to the clean surface or she lets my big brother Ring Abui do it for her. When there is more sesame on a clean surface, my mom grabs a broom and sweeps the sesames into a pile. She scoops sesame into baskets. Not just my mother who did this method, the whole village of Kalthok practiced it; it is the Dinka people culture lifestyle.

Even though there were, no shops around in the village to get body lotions or a baby oil. Perhaps, that did not stop my mother from keep my skin smooth. "How is it smell was not the issue but for smooth skin was the big consideration." She used to make oil out of sesames and seeds of a thoou tree. She had to dry fry whatever she got either sesames or thoou seeds until they turn black then she puts them in what's call Doong in Dinka. It is a mortar that made out of a log. She puts sesames in a mortar while still hot and then she used a pestle to pounds the sesames into dough. After that, she squishes the dough harder with her hands to let the oil out of it. She used that oil to put on my bothers and I when our skins are dry.

Thoou is another very important wild fruits in my home area that people in the village used for food during the food shortage. No one planting this kind of tree, it's just grows by itself anywhere in the area. People drinking juice of a thoou tree and then eat seeds inside of it as well. To get juice out of thoou, just gather the amount you need into a blow then add water to it, mix it together with your hands therefore, that water will turn brown and that is the thoou juice. However, you take the actually shell contain with seeds inside and spread them out on ground in sun to dry and then crake shell of a thoou tree open to get the seeds out of it. These thoou seeds, my mother used to boil them and drain the hot water out, and finally she places them into cold water for a couple of days in order for bitter to fade out of seeds. She drains water again and spread them out in sun to dry for just a minute or two and then these seeds are ready to be eaten. She could mix thoou seeds with sorghum, peanuts, and corn and those taste good indeed.

The dry season is the hardest not just, because it is extremely hot and dry but because by then most of your food is gone. There have been many times when my mother would try to trick us kids by taking a dry bone, boiling it, adding a little salt to it, and calling it soup. It was one drought season where everything was dried and no green plants whatsoever. My people call it "Ruun Maghook" which is meant the year of drought. My mother would do anything to keep us alive and feed us the best she could. She has even gone so far as to make flour out of grass seeds. In my village, there is certain type of grass that got nice seeds. This grass is called Rab ee tit in Dinka. My mother used to cut this grass down and save it for roofing. She did it every year when the grass is growing long. She never knew this grass seeds would save our lives some day. It was just something she improvised at that difficult time. This is also the time when the children are send to the cattle camp where they can at least have milk as a source of food. I can remember one dry season that was especially hard. It was the summer of 1986, there was no rain in Kalthok. No one was able to cultivate that year. There was no food. Many of the trees that grow wild fruits were dying. In Kalthok, there are trees that grow fruits such as Achuil, Kuom, Malkaak and Riath. These fruits are popular snacks for children during hard times when there is little to no food available. During this particular year, the only plant that did not dry up was the Tuk Akot. This tree grows along the river Guar. People would spend nights waiting for the fruit to drop. When it does drop from the tree, it makes a very loud noise and when it is heard, everyone runs to get it. You must be quick. You must wait for the fruit to drop because there is no other way of getting it out of the tree. The tree is very tall and there are no lows enough branches to climb up and pick the fruit. You must also be careful when running to get the fruit. I remember a time when my brother Ring, and our cousin Arechie Nyanpiu where is charge of gathering food for our families. They stayed up all night waiting. Ring and Arechie were fighting over a fruit from a palm tree. Arechie pushed Ring down and he cut his hand on a sharp branch of Tuk, very badly. Because there was no doctor to take care of the wounds, my mother had to do the best she could by keeping the cut clean with warm water just so it would not be infected.

To have a big family is always a dream for people of Kalthok, South Sudan. We believe that having a big family is one of the million ways to become wealthy. In fact, in the Dinka culture the more girls you have, the more cows you will get. A cow, to the Dinka, is a type currency often more important than actual money. To have many boys, is not such a bad thing either. Each boy will grow to have a family of their own, increasing your family line and land. The more people in the village the better; this helps defend the village from outside attacks. The number of wives one man has is another sign of wealth. In order to get married you must pay a dowry to the bride's family, many times in the form of cattle. The more cattle you have, the more wives you can afford.

When a man finds a woman he wants to marry, he must get approval first from his family and then approval from the family of the woman. Typically, no one will refuse the proposal unless that family has a bad reputation. If your family reputation is good, but you don't have enough for a dowry, they will allow the marriage to take place, with the understanding that you will make good on the dowry as soon as you can. If your family reputation is not good, they will refuse the marriage even if you offer a large dowry. A lot of decisions are determining by your family reputation and status within the community. Once the marriage proposal is approve, then the family of the bride will travel to the groom's village to sit down with the elders and discuss the wedding but most importantly agree upon the number of the dowries. During negotiations, it is expect of the groom and his family to host the bride's family. He must make sure they have a place to sleep and also enough food for his visitors to eat. It is expected that of the groom to cover any and all of these expenses. After all negotiations are final, the groom and his family will then travel to the bride's village. There the groom will dance for the bride. This dance is call Kaeny (the wedding ceremony). It is the official acceptance dance of the wedding. When the wedding is finalized, the bride still has one more thing to do. The bride must host a formal dinner for grooms' younger brothers. This gesture is another sign of respect. It is telling them that they are all welcome into their home at any time. This dinner also lets her in-laws know that while they come to the house they are allow and welcome to eat with them. If the bride does not host and offer this first dinner then they will not eat at her house, they do not want to insult the bride.

I remember back home in Kalthok Aliab, South Sudan if a person wants to get married but cannot afford a dowry at the moment then he could make an arrangement to pay the dowry at another time, you must make it. If the man dies before he can makes good on his agreement, that debt is then pass on to his children, if he has any. If he doesn't have any children then it is up to the mans' clan or immediate family to fulfill this obligation. This is what happened to my mother when she married her first husband Abui. He made arrangements with my mother's uncle to pay the dowry at a later time. Unfortunately, Abui died of an illness before he could pay the dowry. It then became the responsibilities of my brothers. When the time can to pay my Uncle, I was already here in the United States and just recently learned that my family was alive and got in contact with them. I sent my brothers some money to help purchase cows for themselves and for a part of the dowry. Once the dowry has been paid in full the wedding is considered officially over now.

My people of Kalthok live by the rule they set for themselves in order to avoid conflict and disorganization especially in cattle camp where everybody needs a cattle campsite to keep his/her cattle herds. This rule applies to everybody in a cattle camp. It just like here in America, but for America, it is all on a business owner of the campground to set the requirements. Whenever you go camping, you always get a campsite to set up your tent. The same as in cattle camp, each person gets a cattle campsite, which is call Gol in Dinka. Gol is where a person leash down his/

her cows on post nicely in a circle. The owner of the Gol has to build some half fen horizontally in the center of the Gol. This half fen is where the children sleep. It protects the kids from unleash roaming cows at night so cows don't step on children or whoever sleeping there.

We love our culture very much and we respect it as well. People pass it on along the line from generations to generations. My people of Kalthok rely on culture for selfcontrol.

It is very hard for a Dinka person to do some thing stupid in the community because he/she knows it will be embarrassment to him/her(self) or to the community.

I was waiting anxiously for my lower teeth to be remove and become young adult.

Unfortunate, that did not happen according to my plan. It was spoil before I even reached age of seven. It was matter of nine months to go so I could start my adulthood process. Whom should I blame for that of missing my culture initiative?

I blame the Khartoum Government for kicked me out of my home. I was looking forward to do a perak process with my age mates. I know that every ethnic group in South Sudan has different ways of processing the adulthood stages. According to Aliab Dinka culture, there are some steps that you have to take in order to become and adult. Removing lower teeth is one of the steps to become an adult.

When a child reached 10 year old then his/her lower teeth have to be removes.

This mean you are considering as teenager who fulfills his/her first step of becomes and an adult. Now the Dinka boys have to do initiative as next steps regardless of becoming young adult. When a boy turns 15 years old then he is ready for initiative stages. The boys of the same ages gather in one place that they chose to stay during the period of the initiative. If they boys of the same ages decided to do initiative, they do it secretly without elders' knowledge about their plan until the process in progress. The woman that the initiatives chose to serve and take care of them whiles staying in her home; she has to use only one razorblade to shave all the initiatives' head. There is no requirement number of initiatives to be in a team. Each Aperak has to make his own metal chain to wear on his neck and a bat to carry around all the time on their roam. At the time of initiation, non of these young men are not allowed to have dairy produces of any kind but just only regular food. That's how the elders set it as the law to belief and obeys in the community. Also, another curiosity behind it is that people think if any of the initiators get hold of cow milk then he could get warts in his body.

The food is prepared by parents in the community and brought over to where the boys are staying. A mother or a sister whose son or brother is in initiative groups will cook especial food for her son every day until the end of program. Whenever the Aperakies go for a walk to the river to take a shower, they walk in one long line one after another from shortest to tallest. This shortest person does every thing first before everyone else. It is the rule of an initiative program that a shortest person is the leader of the group because people consider a short person as a strongest. And they belief he could take care of whatever danger comes across. This short person is like a bodyguard to the team. He is always the first one on line to clear the road from heavy dew on the long grass along the roadside. He is the one responsible for tasting every food that being brought over by parents for the Aperak from the community. Whatever dish taste delicious he keeps that for himself and no one will say anything. No one starts eating until the shortest person says so. In addition, a shortest person is the one goes to bed first before everyone because going to bed for initiatives (Aperak) is a nightmare. A lot of punching in faces and more fighting just to go to bed happened every night during the bedtime. It is a culture belief for Aperak, by doing hard punching on faces of each other will make you become stronger and brave young man.

I was looking forward to wear my set of a corset after I am done with initiative process. Because after initiative process is complete then it is time to move on to next steps of adulthood of which a person wears corsets. Each type of corset can be wear for maximum of two to three-year period.

There are three stages of a corset a man can go through during his manhood after initiative. All these three types of corsets are made up differently. Each of these corsets are set up with different colors of beads. They are combine together and arrange on a piece of metal string nicely aesthetically traditionally way. The young men and girls of the same age wear it on back and around the ribs and stomach.

The first one is Maguel corset. This stage is from 20 to 25-year-old. A maguel corset is made up of white beads in center and black with blue beads around the edges.

The other stage is Ayor corset. The people of age of 30 to 35-year-old wear Ayor corset. This type of corset is made of red beads in a center of it and black beads around the edges.

The last one is Kech corset. It is the last stage that a person stops. Some people decided to wear Kech corset with the next generations even though their generation is fast and retired. Kech is made up of yellow beads in center and white beads next to it. The red and black beads go around the edges.

I had seen here in America and other development countries that a musician needs instruments to make music so the people can enjoy listening to these songs. People wrote songs and documented them in paper or record them on CDs and on social media for a long term used. People can remember these songs as time goes by, from generation to next generations to come. The people of Kalthok, South Sudan does not record their songs on CDs or write them in paper.

Instead, it's all about memorization of the songs you created. You teach the songs to your friends and then release them to the public. By releasing your songs people will hear them during the big dancing day in the village or in cattle camp and that's how the public learns your songs.

I know and it is true that a Dinka man can create many songs base on whatever he has whether it is a colorful bull, Dhuoor/tassel, or looth / big mater bell. I know because I was born there and lived around this people of Kalthok. A person could produce an album praising colorful bull of his interest among the other bulls.

Perhaps, colorful bull is the theme that Dinka men used to created songs. It is very fascinating how Dinka man praises his colorful bull with so many songs. A man could let his brother or any kid from the cattle camp walks his bull around the cattle camp walking behind the kind with bull while singing his songs. A girl please by the songs will take butter and rough gently all over the kid who walking the bull and on bull horns as well. That girl will get very nice praising song about her by the man whose bull had been apply with butter. Dinka man sings many songs about favorite colorful bull to impress the girls and to become a well-known person in the village.

When I was little, I always wish to have my own tassels some day. That was the only thing I always think about and to have colorful cow bull so I can create my songs. It is very common in my village any man wish of own tassels. The Dinka men can make tassels out of cow tails or horse's tail and they called it Dhuoor in Dinka language. They put tassels on a thread rope or on a string with some, colorfully beads add to it in order to make it look pretty. In fact, the songs created base on Dhuoor are different from the one for the colorful bull or Looth/big metal bell. Same as the songs create base on black and white color bull or of any color are also different from a metal bell. Dhuoor/ tassels are another category that Dinka people love to make songs base on indeed. Dhuoor is making out of cow or horsetail. The owner thread tassels on long string and adds some beads on it to make it looks pretty. The owner kept off tassels on his bull's horns most of the time in order to proven tassels from getting lost in woods when the bull is grassing. Unless he decided to go singing in other cattle camp then he has to put tassels on bull's horns. To hook tassels on bull horns, the owner has to punch the hole on a tip of the bull horn, on both horns using fishing rode. Person place fishing rode in fire then push through on a tip of the horn to create a hole.

A big metal bell call looth in Dinka is one of the best lovely instruments that Dinka men like to have in their lives. People can buy this Looth with money or cows from a blacksmith or from other owner. A person own looth has to write songs about a looth instrument. Just only very few people have this rather an instrument, may be one or two looth in a cattle camp. There are not a lot of people who can make this bell, therefore, people buy it from locate a black smith most of the time. The owner used some kind of belt that made out of animals skin to tie looth around his ox. The only time that the owner put on the big bell on his ox neck is when the cattle camp moving to a new place. Looth played a big role in cattle camp. Dinka people using it to remind people in the cattle camp when it is time to relocated cattle camp for better grassing. It is use for messaging communication in cattle.

When all members in cattle camp agreed to go somewhere new for better grassing, then the elders inform the owner of the bell to ring it. There is certain way to ring the bell so people should know its moving time.

As time goes by the moment of happiness, freedom, and fun of playing games and telling the stories shrunk. Living condition became difficult; fear from violent of killing grew more every day. I called it "the end of happy life" that all because of the war between North Sudan regime and Southern Sudanese Government [SALA movement]. This war had been going on for quite some time since before I was not even born. This war took lives of many generations in the last twenty-one years of conflict. Every generation in South Sudan faced the pain caused by "war" that's includes animals and plants. Trees were dry up from pouring down bullets like a raindrop every single day; grasses were fried with human blood. The herbivores' animals become a carnivore and depend on human being for food.

That was due to many human dead bodies everywhere on ground in the battlefield. The loud noise of shooting machine guns scared all the animals faraway to the neighboring countries in Africa and some were dead of poison form machine guns. Therefore, people did not have anything to hunt for food to survive and that made life so harder for my family to survive. Southern Sudanese people never stopped fighting to become a selfgovernment country out of North regimes. The leaders of the Southern Sudan never give up ringing the bell of freedom for the people of South Sudan. They did not like the way Arabs North treated the people of Southern Sudan. They did not like "the idea of forcing someone to follow someone's religion in unacceptable way or by force." Paying someone to wipe out other villages and take children for slavery was way out of our interest! Killing someone for his/her belongings so you can take them away was existing in my home area. Some time I wish there is a medication for hate, I think maybe then people would not do bad things to other human being. The North Sudan had been trying to keep South Sudan in dark for so long as they want. Whenever they saw the "light" on southland, they just want to turn it back off! The south Sudanese leaders never get exhausted or give up of turning the lights back on. They had been kill one after another for speaking out the voice of South Sudanese people. None of these leaders never afraid to step up and said no to more torturing of South Sudanese people. Dr. John Garand de Mabior late former of the SPLA moment finally made the freedom dream for South Sudanese happened in 2005 when peace agreement was sign between North and South. The leaders of the South Sudan who lost their lives were not dying as the fact of the natural death. Theirs lives were taken away by the foes because they were the eyes of the country south Sudan. At right now, none of this will ever happen because south Sudan got her whish, the dream that I been waiting for since that day of revolution. Most important, South Sudan voted for a referendum and became independents country out of North as they wish. It is the great victory that the South Sudanese people should celebrate every year like the rest of the other countries around the world.

Beside, as right now southern Sudan got her own government and a president. Perhaps, southern Sudan is on a map of the world of which she was not exist before.

I witness two attacked conducted by rebels group together with North armies in my present in the year of 1986. They came so many times in the past but there was no serious damage occurred like these two attacks. I went in bush to hide with my family couple of times of rebel attacked. I was maybe four years old when this happened In Nyamot village about ten miles away from Yanguei where I used to live. They came at night when people were sleeping outside in mosquito net and some inside the houses. As soon as they reached the town, they started firing guns at people and set houses on fire. 86 people were kills that night, two children age of four and ten are taken by the rebels; three girls were kidnaped as well.

Perhaps, my cousin Nyajory Machar was one of the victims. They took some of the cows, which were there in a fence in town. Deng Makur was there that night somehow he managed to escape a life after the dip cut on his neck by gang rebels.

According to his statement, he said he played dead when he got hurt. He runs to the cattle camp nearby called Gakaroor to inform people about the attacked.

Then the young men immediately convey the message to other cattle camps by beating drum continually in traditional way of alerting people if there is fighting somewhere in the community. It was too late to go after the rebels they already long gone far enough nowhere to be found. Of cause it was a good thing that they didn't find the rebels otherwise none of the Aliab men wouldn't return because they don't have weapons to fight back just only spears and bats with shields and these weapons would not do any good to a person with a real gun. Belook young men went after the rebels for whole night followed tracks but no sign of them at all. We went to the woods that night to hide after we heard so many noises of the shooting guns continually nonstop. Perhaps, we came back home in the morning but all those times, people were in hiding mood all the times!

Second attacked occurred in Town of Kalthok two years later after the first attacked. This was the time I left Kalthok, South Sudan. Few of the SLPA soldiers were deployed in Kalthok when the gang rebels group together with some of the Arab north armies came back to our village. I do not even think this rebel group got the name of the political party they were fighting for? The Arab North armies did not know their way around in the areas, so they got together with the rebels and then the rebels shown them, where people were living. The Khartoum Government always paid the rebels to kill people for them. They were traveling along the river Guar in the middle of night to Kalthok. Everyone in the town was a slept. Nobody was aware of the attack; soldiers were not out guiding that nights meaning none of them were not prepared to fight back. They surrounded town and started shooting people. Many civilians and soldiers were killed included Riak Chak and a famous person Tol Awuou from Jonglei States.

23

I was sleeping inside the house on a floor while the other members of my family were a slept outside by the door in mosquito net. It was summer time so the weather was a little bit warm. On my sleep, I heard a loud noise of shooting machine guns. I woke up and ran outside then I saw a fire flame of burning houses with thick darker smoke going up straight toward the sky, and so many bullets flew in air like shooting stars. Then as soon I evident the fear hazard, I started running into the woods to hide myself, and for that moment, I never thought of checking on my parents and sibling in mosquito net outside. I decided to keep running far as I could until I reached to Minykaman (Gulyar) town about two hours from kalthok. I did not know if my family runs away to the woods first before me or I was the one who runs first at that time. However, I think I run first; my parents would not just abandon me in the time of situation like that. I never wanted to go back to Kalthok after the tragic attacked because I was afraid that there would be another attack as always. My parents were looking for me worried sick and I was doing the same thing too while I was in Minykaman (Gulyar). From that day, I never talked to my parents face to face until 2009 when I went back home to Southern Sudan for the first time in twenty-one years. People went back home after a couple of days of hiding in woods. Mingkaman (Gulyar) was where I met Peter Keny, Abraham Awolish, Peter Awuol Madier, Araeng Ngor Areng,

Awuor Akech, and Akech Abei Aguok. We both walked together all the way to Ethiopia taking care of one another every step of the ways until Dimma refugee camp, Ethiopia. "Belief in present and hope for the future."

CHAPTER 2

The day I was separate from my family Mingkaman (Guolyar)

Two days after I decided not to go back home to kalthok, I reported myself to Mr. Bior for registration as one of the lost children. Mr. Bior was the SPLA commander who was in charge of the lost children in Mingkaman at that time. There was no something else to do, however, Mr. Bior made me run every morning around the block as part of excise to stay active and avoid being thinking more about home and parents and feel home sick; which was the biggest disease among the lost children who were there in Mingkaman. I played the game of one, two (tok ku row) with some of other lost boys. Also, played soccer some time during the day and then go for a swim in the river Nile to cold off from long ran in hot sunny day.

There was no school to go to in Mingkaman because everybody lived in fear. I used to watch anglers unload their boat full of fish on the shore every day in the morning and in the afternoon. Watching the anglers on the shore with wood boat and fish was quite fascinating. It was like watching favorite TV show on television.

The people of Mingkaman made contribution of fish and sorghum every week to Mr. Bior to feed all the lost children with these food supplies. After the attack in Kalothok, I saw some parents brought in theirs children to Mr. Bior for protection and to go to school where is safe. Mingkaman was the place where I started to live alone and took care of myself.

I do not remember how long I live in Mickman but long enough to move onto different place. I was afraid of living there due to some reasons: I was tired of waking up supper early in the morning every day to go for a run, which I did not have to do when I was at home in Kalthok. I was always afraid that the rebels would attack me again in Mickman village and that was my biggest fear ever. My concept was to just move far away, as I could, God known where but elsewhere out of the country. I never got my full sleep since the day I left Kalthok; too much night mares. I was skeptical of going for a walked in a village side. I was always afraid and thought that the rebels were in woods.

Next morning when the bodyguards woke me up I thought I was going for morning run as usual routine, but it was the time to move to the next step to the safety shelter. Gathered whatever you had, your belongings and go on shore said,

Mr. Bier. You are going to Aeneid the Bor. Town on the other side of the river Nile said, Mr. Bier. I heard about Bor. before but never been there, of cause it is on the other side of the river Nile. I was so excited to hear that statement thinking I was finally had to move onto a different place even though I did not know what head of me was. They loaded us in anglers' boat that made out of wood. It took me a complete day to reach to the other side of the shore because of the heavy current wave that make the boat goes slowly. It was about around six o'clock in the evening when I get to the other side of the River Nile. I walked from the shore to the place where I was supposed to be staying. They waited until everyone was there then we head down the road in single line to Anyitdi town in Bor, jonglei state.

CHAPTER 3
Anyidi

At that time, the SPLA Government was my food provider and at the same time they were my protectors as well through out of my entire journey all the way to Ethiopia. Since the SPLA did not have enough food of their own to feed me in Anyidi town therefore, the SPLA officials made the community contributed sorghum for the other lost children and I included to eat. The community has to give cows, goats, and dry fish or whatever they have for food. Unfortunately, the community did not contribute meat of any kind at all except fish and sorghums.

That year was really, bad indeed, because as I moved along to Anyidi, all I saw were dead cows everywhere lying down on the roadside. The epidemic disease breaks out cause by poison on grasses from the machine's gun during the war.

Many people died from this poison. I do not know for sure what it was but I think it was something to do with the weapons that were used by Northern forces during the war between SPLA and the Khartoum Government.

When I reached to Anyidi, the officials showed me where I would be staying for time being while waiting for the other lost children from others villages to come.

There was no a house or a hut built for us to temporally live in. perhaps, the SPLA officials were not aware of the number of the lost children who were coming to Anyidi town. However, due to the large number of the lost children, the town leaders and SPLA officials decided to resettle us under the trees in wood outside of the town in order to avoid conflicts with people of Anyitdi. I stayed under the trees during the daylight and sleep in an open area at night so the guard can have a better view to protect us at night from Nyanjuan and rebels. The fear of foes and a wild small animal called Nyanjuan was terrifying the people of Anyidi just like people of Kalthok with fear of Arab north forces. This animal creature eats small children and young adults; to fast over night to the next morning was a wish good luck. The SPLA soldiers had to guard the camp from

27

Nyanjuan the whole night. "It didn't matter how early it was as soon as the sun set, that mean no more movement except to stayed foot in my sleeping spot."

Even when I was in Mingkaman (GulyAR), Mr., Bior warned me to be careful and not to roam alone at night because of Nyanjuan. Getting water to drink or to cook with was a struggling; I had to walk miles and miles to the river to get water, which was not funny at all. I thought moving onto a new place will changed my fear a bit; however, I was underestimating the true meaning of a mystery! It turns out that the people of Anyidi were in fear of their own too like I was in Kalthok.

There were good numbers of lost children across the villages resettling in Anyidi town. This town of Anyidi was the checking point for people who were looking forward to the safety shelter just like me. The SPLA officials had to check to make sure no very sick children in the crowds. These children have to be left a side and not to move on with crowds until they are fully recovering. My cousin Madit Nyedong was one of the sick children who were put a side by the SPLA officials in Anyidi, to regain his strength and get healthy before he moved on journey. My motivation was just to keep going forward and not looking back, however, even though I feel sick I act normal as like a healthy kid so the officials do n't make me stays behind. The officials started contributed some sorghums to everyone that evening. I did not know what was behind of it, I thought it was just the part of the contribution activities as usual. Whatever that day was? It was the day my sorrow increased more all the way to Ethiopia. It was the day that I stepped over a slaughtering bull.

This was the day I started to step out of the South Sudan's boarder line to a neighboring country, Ethiopia for safety. In my whole entirely journey, some time when I close my eyes, I visualized that morning when the elders of Anyidi town slaughter a bull and made everyone walked over it falling in single line of crowds. It was the sign of blessing because according to Dinka culture, when a person is going somewhere unknown or a place that he/she never been to before.

The elders have to do that kind of activity of slaughtering goat, sheep, and cow as the way of saying goodbye and have a safe journey and may God bless you on your tripe.

This was the day I heard the sound of whistle blowing for the second time. A whistle never stops screaming until I reach to Ethiopia Dimma refugee camp.

However, it did not bother me at all until later on along the path as I continuing nonstop on a journey to Ethiopia. The purpose of blowing a whistle was to remind the crowds that It's time to move on, so if someone is away from the camp at that movement, then a blowing whistle will remind him/her to come back and get ready for the road. It was good they came up with the idea of whistle blowing communication to reminded people when it was time to go otherwise most of the people would have been left behind. I always went out to look for something to eat in every town the refugees stopped in to rest. However, whistle blowing was my reminder plus my group mates, but I can hear them when they yell out for my name because some time it too loud to hear someone calling for your name. Most of the SPLA soldiers remain in Anyidi, some of them were select to scout the travel refugees to Ethiopia, and Mr. Commander Amiemdit was the head of the scout. It was dark when I got to the next resting area: the Sarah of Ajaker. There were so many people, children, older people, and women with the babies. Therefore, to find your group mates or town mates was hard. Therefore, if you are the first one arrive to the resting area then it is that first person's responsibility to make sure everyone in his/her town or villages to find the way to under the tree or any open spot of his choice. You have to yell aloud the name of your town for, e.g., Kalthok or Anyidit and so on. There was no post made with the name of town or village on it to hold up so the people of that town or village could see and come to the name sign. However, due to insecurity reason, the safety seekers (the travel refugees) do name-calling during the daylight but not at night.

At night, you can sleep wherever you land together with other people. The rebels also afraid of attacking the refugees at daylight, the hided themselves as well.

I was about to step into different territory of young gang rebel groups. This people were not participate in political game or anything else. They were not even fighting for freedom or something else but for their own interest of cattle and culture initiative reasons. They do not even have a name of political party movement. This young gang rebel group always got their weapons from other people they killed or on a black market and from Khartoum Government. "This rebel groups train themselves to kill!" According to theirs, expect, if a person killed many people then that person become famous in community. However, this person could get tattoos base on number of people he killed. Perhaps, for this young gang groups killing was like some kind of tradition cultural activities for them.

In fact, these two rebel groups of Taposa and Murlei do not get along at all; they fight all the time over cattle and territory. I remember one person by name Lopir from Taposa tribe. He was in Pakok refuge camp, South Sudan in 1991 in Dikdik group of Young children. He was one of my caretakers who were appointed t by the SPLA officials to look after the minor Dikdik group. He was my best friend. "His right eye was missing which made me wonder of what happen to his eye!" One day I asked him about his eye. He did not hastate or got an embrace when I ask him that question if he could tell me about what happened to his missing eye. In fact, he was so proud of it. He told me that his right eye was removing for better aiming on target he wanted to shoot. He did not want to close his eye every time he puts a gun on his right shoulder to aim at the target and then shoot in a clear rage. Therefore, he let his right eye removed for automatically aiming set up purposes. He told me much more about his culture and that how I knew the reason of many tattoos all over his body.

CHAPTER 4
Sarah of Ajakeer

Fourth day of the journey to a place I called "the hope to catch a breath from danger." It started to rain as I head the road around four o'clock in the morning from Ajaker to Nyinkongkong. I was carrying some water and a little bit of food contributed by the SPLA representatives in Anyidi town for the road, which did not last me half way to Dimma camp, Ethiopia. Peter keny, Peter Awoul Madier, Akech Abei, Awuor Akech, Areng Ngor, Abraham Awolish, and I were group mate, we were walking together, taking care of one other on the way to safety. I thought it would rain all the way to Nyinkongkong the next distention. The SPLA commander who was in charge of escorting the travel refuges or the safety seekers to safety told crowds to empty out water containers. There will be a lot of water along the way to Nyinkongkong; you will be walking in a rain flood said the commander Amiedit. The crowds did as he said and empty out water canes. The commander thought that there would be water along the way up to next stop. His concept was to reduce the weight of luggage that people were crying but he did not know the rain stop half way to Nyinkongkong. After a couple of miles walking in muddy rain: the dry land approach where no any rain drops whatsoever.

Everyone became exhausted and hungry from a long walk in muddy rainwater.

Some group of people decided not to proceed on a journey to Nyinkongkong, however, they return to Ajaker so the can waited for the rain to stop. Thus, worth case scenarios, the SLPA commander who was in charge and who told people to get rid of water got affected by exhaustion, hungriness, and thirstiness right away when he reached the dry area, he walked behind with his bodyguards to make sure nobody left behind alone. After the coincidence situation, Mr. Amiedit's bodyguards run to the resting area to fetch water for him. In fact, that was the time I became home sick, I was thinking about my mother and father and I was very anxious to get to a final destination so I do not have to walk anymore. I even called her name out in low sleepy whispering voice, "mother!" Where are you? I called my mother's name while zooming out walking side to side across the road without anything underneath my feed and without light to see in dark, it was dangerous! "God known what was on that side of the road or on that road I was walking on for that mater." I didn't hear a responded voice of yes my child when I yelled out calling the name mommy and daddy. I was in pain at that moment so I called my parents to comport me unfortunately they were not there at the time I need them. I used to run to my mother or father to comport me when I am hurt.

They used to kiss my hurting spot, clean my nose and my eyes from dirt every second in a day and night. Now I am on my own doing everything by myself and I didn't even have strength to do them all. I didn't know what would go to happen to me on the journey to Ethiopia without my parents beside me. "I was, like a blind person who doesn't have an idea what is on ground in front. But to keep going until he feels what exactly on ground in front and then he has to make decision of what direction to turn." "I lost the feeling of calling the name mommy and daddy for cheering up in time of sorrow." I do not know any more how its feel like to used word mommy or daddy in time of need. Before it was amazing, I always feel happy when I called my mother or father when I am hurt. They respond to my call, hug me, and hold me up on their arms. At right now, those feelings are not there anymore because the war storm washed them away out of my mind. I do not think I will gain that feeling back in me it is far-gone forever. I just want to be strong and live with it. That what I had been doing anyway for the last 21 years without my parents. "Beside I am already a grown up man so it would not be matter anyway to call my mother or daddy for cheering up as like when I was still a baby."

I was so tired and sleepwalking alone between the cut off lines of groups of people matched up walking two, 3 or 5 to 10 the most. My mouth and throat were dried with a crake on bottom and top of my lips to the point I couldn't' even slowed a spit. I tried everything I could to keep me going with crowds. I dung ground with my bar hands just to grab wet dirt and suck on it to attract at least a little bit of spit into my mouth. I breathe in and out with my mouth wide open for cold air to engage my mouth and throat but it made my mouth even drier. No spit at all in my mouth but only just the dry air engages my mouth. Then the last thing I tried was drinking my own urine though no much came out of me it was worth a try. I didn't even remember how I came up with these ideas, I guest when you are struggling to survive at the time of hardship, the all crazy ideas always gather in your mind.

I have seen so many scary things that I never saw before in my life on this adventure journey to safety. Everywhere I looked on the roadside the only thing I could see were human skeletons and fresh dead bodies file up in form of a hill.

There were Vultures everywhere tearing apart human bodies for food. Foxes, hyenas, loins, wilds, and so many other animals that want to eat human being were there following me. The vultures were following people around which scary me a lot! Seeing a bird follow you over was a terrified situation. When I approach to something like that, it gave me Goose bumps and the hair in my headstand up straight and my eyes pop out. I was so frighten for the whole situation at that moment. And from that moment, my fear rises from the hiding place inside me. I was so afraid I thought I would going to die there. However, it didn't defeat me; I close my eyes and keep moving forward with the crowds. At first, my biggest fear was that, if I am not strong enough to make it through to the other side I will die here and my bones will be among these dead people. Before in Anyidi town, I heard some people-talking bout the ghost on the way to Nyinkongkong, that they call your name and want you to join them. Therefore, as I moved along. I remembered that statement and that make me not to be alone and away from the crowds, I just want to keep up with the crowds. The smell in the desert never changes even at night when the temperature change to a moderate cold air; still the same as it is daylight. The dry airs with a lot of dust going spin every second caused so much eye problems that almost makes me go blind due to the pink eye I had which caused by too much dust in the desert. It wasn't the energy in my body that kept me going but God was there on my right shoulder. My strength, my heart, and my mind were the emergency power backs up which sent the strong encouragement to my whole body. I did not know where I was going. I was like a robot, controlled by a remote control, running around across the road in zigzags on the road of Ajaker! I asked myself every day even to this day; "How did I make it out alive on that terrible road at the age of six without parents?"

CHAPTER 5
Nyinkongkong

"Not even a full day" and the whistle scream reminding people to pack their things and moved onto the next stop area which I didn't even know the name of it until later that day when I reached to the place!, It was pibor town. It was after the sun set when I fell in line of crowds matching on trail track to Pibor town, the next stopping point.

I didn't get a chance to look around the area. I never have times to find out what was there in that place or know how big the area was? Instead, the only thing I worried about was to get water and make myself a dinner before I move onto the next town. Thanks God! Nyinkongkong, the resting area was on the river, "a small river in the middle of no where! Without a cannel branch that coming out of the ocean or any big lake." Who knows how clean those waters in that river were?

However, I didn't care about the hygiene. The only thing I cared about was to cook my Sorghum, eat and then get some eye shot because I have to take advantage of that pausing movement of time. However, to cook something was a challenge due to insecurity in the area. Therefore, I had to dug the hole under the ground, put dry sticks underneath, light them up with a fire and then put another row of thick wood on top of the first dry stick. Finally add just little bit of dirt on top of the wood just to reduce smoke from raising up high then I place my cooking pot on top of the dirt; so basically, I was using warm steam dirt to cook my sorghum with.

To cook the sorghum well done, wasn't the biggest concern but as long the water is warm enough to heat up my sorghum, that's all I need. Whatever left over, I put it in a linen bag for the next time meal.

There was no sign of civilization in Nyinkongkong, it was just like a deer camp where everyone pasting by take, making a quick stop and do their things before they move onto the next town.

"The journey was nothing but the military training camp." "It was a mater of life and death!" Every shift in a day got its problem. "At daylight, I hide myself from rebels not to kill me." The gang rebels killed very good number of people a head of me and people who came after me. Those rebels were just cattle herders like other cattle keepers in South Sudan but the Khartoum Government mobilized and gave them guns. During night time I had to be careful where I want to be because there were wilds animals everywhere in wood that kill human being for food, a lion being one of them. It became harder and harder every second of the day.

Every footstep I took was painful indeed. Too many long hours on foot without enough sleep made me so tired. The luck of body comfort rest, also, starvation and dehydration were the main factors of my life at that movement. All bad things affect life such as sorrow, depression, and anxiety accumulated inside me and tried to drags me down almost to the hell. Thus, I didn't give them a chance to pull me down; I trip on rocks and land down on my face but never thought of giving up. "I kept trying over and over again without wear off my hope! That, one day I will get there." Most of my friends did not follow my secret of survival and that why most of them did not makes it to Ethiopia. "How did I make it out alive? I ask myself that question every single day."

It was before I reached to Pibor Town when I heard the news from one of the SPLA soldiers about the attack conducted by the gang rebels in Nyinkongkong. The victims were the remainders patients in Anyidi town who were left behind to get better and be able to resist the obstacles on the way, together with other more safety seekers/the travel refuges. They left from Anyidi after a couple of days of their recovery from sickness. The rebels ambush this group of people as they leave Nyinkongkong to Pibor. Many of the safety seekers/ the travel refuges were killed that is including small children, the women with little babies on theirs arms, and the women with unborn babies in theirs belly. "Again, I escaped that human slaughtering on that day." From that day, more fear increases among the safety seekers/the travel refuges. It makes even more difficult that no one wants to go first to lead the crowds to safety even the soldiers didn't want to go first.

CHAPTER 6
Pibor

I did not see any civilians in Pibor town when I past through even the soldiers' families, just only the SPLA armies were living there. Is there any reason why only the soldiers live in Pibor town? I did not ask that question and I did not ask why there were no women and children in Pibor town because that was not the thing in my mind to worry about at all during that time.

I sat down under a tree outside of the town where they put me, to rest for a couple of hours, before I moved onto the next stop. I was boiling some maize given to me by one of the soldiers in Pibor town. I was on my knees bending to the ground blowing through the fire with air from my mouth. When I lift my head up from the ground, then I saw a white woman walking among the safety seekers/ the travel refuges with some SPLA officials. Of course, my eyes were watering from smoke fire and my head was spinning from long time blowing through the fire with air from my mouth. I guess she was one of the UN agency person comings from Ethiopia camps to see us. I do not know all these questions pop up in my mind. I followed her around Just to look at her; I did not care what they were talking about. I could not understand any way. That was my first time ever to see a person with different color than myself. From that movement, I was fascinating with the new look among us.

Thanks goodness there was thou/the lalop tree on the way from Pibor to Ponychalla. This plant trees save lives of a thousand of people including myself otherwise, without it the good number of people wouldn't have made it to Ethiopia camps, "even though some didn't make it anyway!" due to Hunger, exhaustion, thirsty, home sick, wild animals attacked, and Murlei rebels attack.

The only sides affect for this thou tree/lalop is too sweet and if you eat too much of it, it would cause you diarrhea!

Some children refused to walk because theirs feet were nothing but a wound underneath. Thus, they were unable to walk and on top of it, they were thinking of parents. I was in the same situation but I looked at other kids who were just like me walking without any weakness on their faces so I did the same thing too as like them. My feet were punctured and cracked with wound underneath. I used to wear animal leather and leaves of a tree to protect my feet from sharp dry mud and thorns along the way.

Another long night journey from Pibor to Ponychalla was painful and exhausting a journey. Pibor was not the final destination I thought it would be. The sun rose before I reached to pochalla. Therefore, I stopped in savanna land to hide for the day from Murlei rebels. There were few trees around spread out distant from one tree to another. I did use some of these trees for shade. I also those trees to hide from rebels. The travel refuges/safety seekers waited until it was dark to head on the road again so the rebels do not see us. That day after the sun sat, the commanders' bodyguards slaughtered two bulls given to the travel refuges/the safety seekers by the SPLA soldiers in Pibor for the road. The bodyguard contributed meat to all the travel refuges, each person end up with a little bit piece of meat. Then later that night the travel refuges left savanna land to pochallla. On the way to Ponychalla, one person Madul from my Aliab tribe got sick unexpectedly and died. It just happened in a mater of a couple of hours. He never showed any sign of sickness when he left town of Pabir.

CHAPTER 7

Ponychalla

As I past through the town to where I was told to be resting, I saw children running around playing on the open field in the middle of town. I thought they were pasting by like myself but they were not; they live there with theirs families.

Some of these families were soldiers' families who were deploying in Ponychalla during that time of war.

Two days after I got to Ponychalla, they told me I was going to Dimma camp,

Ethiopia. Some of the lost boys went to Pinyudo camp, Ethiopia and the rest of other travel refuges myself included went to Dimma camp. Ponychalla was like a conjunction where everybody has to go on his/her way of destination. It was not my wish to choose the refugee camp; the SPLA officials told me where to go to stay. There were many refuge camps in Ethiopia: Dimma camp, Pinyudo, and Itang. All the refuges from South Sudan went to these three different camps in Ethiopia in separated ways. The people who were coming from Nuer area went to Itang at least the good number of Nuer tribe people went there than Pinyudo and Dimma camp because it was closer way for them to get there.

The SPLA officials had to break down the number of refuges into groups and then sent them to these different camps.

Since no one among the safety seekers knew how to get to Dimma refuge camp, Ethiopia, The SPLA commander who was in charge of Ponychala and Anyuak chief selected two Anyuak men to lead the Refugees to Dimma camp, Ethiopia. Amiem dit, the escort leader warned travel refuges about Anyuak people, not to roam around the community far long. They can kill you and ties you to the tree to trap a tiger, said Amiem dit. That was his advice to everybody especially the lost children like myself who didn't have parents. However, that statement scared me the most and not let me wanted to walked far away from the rest area

CHAPTER 8
Anyuak territory

As I moved along through Anyuak territory, it seems the Anyuak people were not bad people after all. Anyuaks people are human beings just as everybody else and they do care about another human being too. The cares of a mother always about her baby and not want anything to happen to her baby appeared on Anyuaks women's faces, they shed "tears" when they saw me walking alone without a mother or a father that far.

However, a non of this statement stated by Imam dit did not ever happen during me merge to Ethiopia. The Annex people were my food providers. Not just me but everybody else those were in the same conditions as I was. When I asked for something to eat the Annex people provided me with food or water, whatever I asked for. However, I was caution though of whatever I received from Annex people. I was afraid they would poison me so I let them taste first anything that they gave me to make sure is save before I go ahead and eat it. I did not know how to speak Annex language, I communicated with them using sign language. My hands were translators, I used them to convey a message of what I need by pointing at something. Anyuak culture was something that I learned when I pasting through to safety of Ethiopia. I was impresses with the way Annex people cultivated theirs corps exactly like Dinka people. At that movement it's remind me about my home soil, so rich anything you put in it comes out exactly just the way you wanted it. Moving through the greenly corn on cup and millet with long stems and fresh leaves waving by wind making hissing sound, make me relax and come.

It was scary to go through those corn and sorghum field but did not bother me a bit. I thought I was back to Kalthok, southern Sudan where I left. Looking at the sorghum gardens for such some long mills distance made my hunger, exhaustion, and missing home motional Disappeared. I was imagining in my mind just as if I was in my mother's sorghum garden walking through with a big smile on my face.

I stopped fourth time before I reached to Rhad the boarder of Southern Sudan and Ethiopia. Every stops I made the Anyuaks people always have to contribute some food for the whole travel refugees just the same routine when I was in Anyidi town.

There was something I learned from Anyuak people about their relationship with other neighbor tribe. The Anyuaks people had the same issue with Murlei tribe over the cattle. The Murlei tribe took all the cattle of the Anyuak people. The Anyuak in general is a big tribe and they have conflict with two tribes: Murlei tribe and Lashipo tribe in Ethiopia. The Anyuak tribe lives between ponychalla and Rhade fight with Kachipo tribe and the other Anyuak tribe live between Pibor and Ponychalla were dealing with Murlei tribe.

Maybe that why I did not see any cows in Annex villages on my way through, they did give up keeping cattle to avoid conflict or they never have any cattle at all? That is I do not know.

That night when the Catchup attacked Annex people was the time I believed what exactly was going on between this two tribes. It was a sad night for Annex people.

Many of them were kills by Catchup. That was another deadly rebel attack I dodged that day. The Kachipo rebels verily missed the place where I was spend the night that day. The travel refuges heard the news in the morning about the attacked conduced by Kachipo rebels. Everyone was in the same situation which was happen in Nyinkongkong when Murlei rebels ambush the refuges thus, no one want to go first. All the refugees were afraid, thinking that Kachipo rebels might ambush the crowds. I did not want to spend another night in that area. My goal was to keep moving onto where I was going. The attack that night never stopped the travel refugees to go to Rhad town, which was the next destination before reaching the final stop. The journey from Ayuak territory was turn out good not ambush attack occurred except some road problems such as thirsty, hunger, exhaustion, and wild animals attack as usual.

CHAPTER 9
Jebel Rhad

It was dark when I get to Rhad town, the boarder of Southern Sudan and Ethiopia.

I spend just a day there and I moved onto where I was going, which was Dimma camp, Ethiopia. I thought I was going straight to Dimma camp from Rhad but I did not know. I stopped in Marcas town before I go to Dimma. That was another small town between Jebel Rhad and Dimma camp. There were no civilians in this town of Marcase just only SPLA soldiers were living there. It was the military training camp. There was no much food to eat in Jebel Rhad and that was one reason I spend just a day there.

That morning when I was arriving to Marcas, I was so hungry and thirsty.

Everywhere on, ground was maize. "Therefore, the word expiration, stains, and dirty was not in my consideration for the maize on ground beside the road." As soon as I spot the corns on the ground, I started to bend down to the ground and pick them up. Then I rushed to where a fire was to make some popcorn by putting maize in a hot ash. I was just going with whatever came first and I saw corns first so I go with it and decided to find water later on.

The SPLA soldiers were yelling at me not to grab food off the floor and they were even-dump out the corns off my hands that any of I picked. Jech Amer! (Red Army) stopped picking up the food off the ground there is plenty of cook maize, said the SPLA soldiers. I did not care what the soldiers said I made popcorn anyway. I had lots of stomach pain from eating too much popcorn on top of other junk food, which I shouldn't have done for the first time with empty stomach.

From that day my belly hurt thus, I had very bad diarrhea for a couple of days then the pain goes away.

The movement of my arrival to Maracas, I feel like the long walk come to an end, indeed it was for those four years I spend in Ethiopia. One last whistle screams again, All the new arrivals gather over there we have a meeting, said the SPLA commander. Welcome to Marcase town, I am very happy that you people made it out life through from that long walked in a desert, said the SPLA commander. Now not of all you will go to Dimma camp, we are going to make some selection among you said the SPLA commander. The older will remain here to be train as soldiers and the women and Jech Amer (the red army or young one will go to Dimma camp, said the SPLA commander. After the SPLA commander stops talking, the soldiers spread out among the refuges to select out the orders people. It was the whole day process, so I decided to go and site down under the shad. My legs were numb and my whole body was shaking because I was very weak from previous walking. I had this issued every time when I stop to rest; then start over always the problem.

Following morning, the SPLA commander let the women and young boys left to Dimma camp; I was one of these boys. It was a slow journey from Macas to Dimma camp, no fear of foes and no scout teams. It is a big and clear road so no need of navigator and security guards. In fact, Dimma camp was not far away from Marcas; however, we took our time to go slowly by just milking it all the way to Dimma.

CHAPTER 10

My first refugee camp in Dimma refugee camp, Ethiopia

When I was arrived to Dimma camp from Marcase, the UNHR agency and SpLA officials were waiting for me at the end of the road with water and nutrient food on their hands. The UN agency persons gave me little bit of water to drink and if I tried to drink too much water at once. She then took water away from me. The United Nation High Commissioner's for Refuges Person explains it to me why she did not want me to drink too much water at once. Due to lack of enough food in your stomach for so long your intestines shrunk and if you tried to drink too much water at once that may cause you a bell problem, said the UNHCR worker person. She told me to Just take in a little bit at a time will get my digestion system back to normal routine of processing. From that day I was under UNHCR's care for a couple of months before they moved me to my new home.

A week in recovering a center, the Sudan people liberation army (SPLA) together with United Nation High Commissioner for Refuge (UNHCR) did another screening again just likes the one they did in Marcas. They separated young the lost boys out of the people with their families and place them far away from the community groups. Perhaps, I was one of the lost boys. In fact, it was the SPLA officials' idea to put minors in a group so they can keep an eye on them in one place. Another reason was that, I guess they did not want the lost boys to be in the community without anybody to look after them.

I do not remember the date or the month that I came to Ethiopia but I do remember the year though, it was 1988. There were good number of Sudanese refuges already living in Dimma camp when I got there. The weather in Dimma camp was nice not too cold and not too hot just moderate. It's rain every other day in during the week. Therefore, most of the people cultivated okra plus other vegetables. As the days fast by my emotional depression, start to fade away slowly. I was able to show my teeth again for the first time for a long time. Even though there was still unhealed, scars spot in my heart and in my mind, that did not stop me from smiling when I was in a better mood. I started to play some soccer games with my friends between the houses' blocks that we built with grass on roof top and mud wall after got to Dimma camp, Ethiopia. "Playing these, games made me forgot thinking too much about my family." I always join the groups and tell the stories to ourselves every day. This was the way we prevent being lonely and thinking more about home, which was sometime resulting to serious illness. Playing soccer games and telling stories was the only thing we do whole day long before I started school.

In my new home where they put me to stay, the UNHCR set up a feeding clinic facility center where I had meal three time a day all healthy food and drink. TheUN agency person in charge had to select out the very sick children and gave them ID card to get meal at the feeding clinic center three times a day. I was one of these skinny sick children who were given the ID card to get care from the hospital. The people who cook food for these children had to ring the bell when it is time to be serves then we all got in single line to receive a plate of food. I used to bring left over food back to the houses for my friends who did not get a chance to get an ID card. "For some reasons the caretakers in feeding a clinic center do not allow us to bring food back to the group. I do not know why but that was their policy. I had to sneak out some left over food for my friends." The UN person has to weight us every two weeks to check if any of us gain weight or still not gaining weight. And if they found any child with loose weight then they took him/her to Dimma big hospital to be admitted. They do this process so the other kids can have a chance to get healthy food and drink such as BB5 biscuits as well.

Thanks God! Mother Azor dit was there in Dimma camp otherwise, most of us the lost boys would have wounds on them for very a long time without healing. She took the role of motherhood for the lost boys, that was included old and new arrival children. I called her mother Azor dit. I do not even know her really actually full names; the only name stuck in my head is mother Azor dit. In deed, she was the mother of mothers. She was representing the love of all mothers who were not there in Dimma camp to the lost children of the South Sudan. Because of her love, care, and pity every lost boy's wound was healing. I think that why Dr. John Garang selected her to look after the lost children of South Sudan, which he called them the seeds of the new country, South Sudan. No mater how bad your wounds were smell, whether the wounds were full with puss, and the flies' eggs, which exactly my wounds were. She never turns her eyes away from your pain, she sat down and cleans them and then dress your wounds. She even used her own belonging to cloth us when the UN agency did not come soon with supplies.

She always took us to the river to wash off dirt in our body and wounds to stay clean. She even sat down and dug out pleas underneath our feet.

I remember when I was in Dimma refugee camp, Ethiopia in 1990. I did not have many clothes or shoes to change into every day. I wore one per of clothes repeatedly for a long time. Therefore, I had lice accumulated in my clothes and my hair. I did not know other way to get rid of lice out of my clothes and in my hair. I used to place my clothes on ground in sun then applied warm sand on them in order to kill lice. When no razorblade to shape my head. I used can of soda to comb my hair. I punched little holes underneath of that soda can and then put burning coracles inside of it and I rubbed it gently back and forth in my hair. It kills some lice and makes my hair look nice a little bit. After that method I be coming lice free for a couple of days. I added oil in my hair when I comb it to make it straight backward.

In Dimma refugee camp, Ethiopia, the UN does not distribute clothes more often but only food. People buy their own clothes and shoes but for person like me who did not have money to buy whatever I need, always had a problem with lice because I had one pair of cloth. I have to Waite for UN to give me more clothes whenever they are ready to distribute because the UN does not do contribution of clothes and shoes more often in Dimma camp.

One month is gone and I still wondering when am I going to start school? I was a head of myself to think about school that day. Instead, they put me in the military training camp with the other lost boy. The training last a year then I graduated.

During that day of gradation, the SPLA commander Dr. john Garang was there, he was the one conducting ceremony. The soldiers spread out among the graduate students to pick out the strong men to be deployed in front line. The soldiers shook and pushed harder a person that they spot so that to make sure he could hold the guns well. At that time most of us wanted to go to front line to fight for the country so badly, but the leader of the SPLA government Dr. John de Garang Mabior did not want the little boys to go to war instead he wants them to focus on education as theirs duty to fight for the country of South Sudan. Jersh Amer!

Your time will come; you are the seeds of the new South Sudan, just concentrate on school, said Dr. John Garang. Take education under control as your fight, said Dr. Garang. However, everywhere he goes and every meeting he conducted with jersh Amer (the red army), this is the statement he keeps repeated saying to all young lost boys of the South Sudan.

After the SPLA officials got the number of soldiers they want out of the graduates, they break down the remaining graduates into three groups. Marekrek group was the group of all young adults of age of 15 to 18. Jesh al athuot was a group of 19 year old and older. Then the Dikdik groups which was my group was all young boys of 5 to 14 years old. Mading Deng was my caretaker of the Dikdik group and Mr. Duach dit was the assistant. Duach dit does all the fathers' duty of giving advices to young minors of the Dikdik group. Duach also was responsible for the food we eat; he had to make sure that there was enough food for everybody. If any one of us got sick, Duach dit was the one to bring that person to the doctors.

We were too young to cook our own food thus, the SPLA government selected some adult men to cook our food and Duach dit was the one to make sure that the food is cook well. Every thing we needed, Duach dit had to let Mading knows the head caretaker.

During the night time, I slept on a floor in the open field in front of our houses we built. The field was nothing but only hard dry floor without grasses. Where we slept, each person got his own spot to set up his sleeping bag. The UNHCR agency contributed some blanket to all the refugees in Dimma camp. However, there were always many thieves roam at night to rob people with money and some valuable items such as blanket and mosquito nets." One night I set up my blanket at the end of the line in field toward the houses. Then at midnight after everybody a sleep, the group of men came and pulled out my blanket off me and they run away with it for good. These thieves men were depriving of stealing people's blanket every night all over across the camp. "They did this all the time because of the money purposes." That morning I reported the accident to Duach dit and then Duach dit reported to Mading Deng the head caretaker so I could get new blanket otherwise I would have nothing to sleep on. It always took a long time to get new blankets from the UN.

Now I am able to go to school after the training was over. I was so excited and I could not wait to be in class when they told me I was going to school soon when the school open the next season, which was January of 1990. My First day of school was not that bad because what I did was just registration and they showed me the classroom where I want to be. That was my first time ever to attend school so nothing was easy for me at all. The teachers were very hard on me and I did not know anything about alphabetical letters or math for that mater so it was frustrating moment for the teachers as well. Thus, we spend most of our times outside sitting down on ground on our bottoms and a teacher have to tell us what letter to write down on sand using our fingers. If you do not get it right then a teacher, can grab your middle finger and rub it harder on a sand try to show you how to write that letter of the day. However, we spend half of the school year outside writing on sand before we were even given notes book and pens to write with. The only subjects they taught me were only English, math, and Arabic. When a teacher speaks Arabic or English on front of the class I just enjoy the hiss sound that comes out of his/her mouth because, I had no clue what the teacher was talking about? It was hard for me to understand any of the English words or Arabic whatsoever for that first year. Second year of school was better because over the school break I practice reading some of the preschool books, English and math.

Which very much I was suppose to be reading any way but because of my age the teachers did not really care about my grad level and what level to put me in. The first word sentence that my teacher taught me during that first period of school semester was cocologubongochai mataliwa. I did not actually know what this word sentence mean even now I still do not know the meaning of it. I think it was the word from Amharic the Ethiopian language I am not sure for real. This is the only word all students practicing spelling by write on ground in sand every day after school.

School system was very strict on attendant and homework however, when you come late to school in the morning thus, you got hand lashes for being late. The same as home work policy, you got beat for not doing your homework. In class when a teacher ask you a question and not get it right then he/she punish you by using a ruler to hit your fingers and knuckles, teachers do not do buttock lashes only polices did that kind of punishment in Dimma camp. School was very supportive and cheerful to students of all grades however, when a student got good grades on top of all school thus, he/she gets a boxes of bar soap plus other valuable items as the gift for her/she hard work and concentration. I knew this because one of my group mate Atem got good grades on top of all school so he got gifts.

The life in Dimma camp was nice and peaceful for the last four years I spend there.

No fear of danger of foes and no hunger, just only the fear of government control.

No tribalism conflicts among the communities but only peaceful neighborhoods.

All the communities of different dialects from south Sudan were mix up which really made living in Ethiopia camp more peaceful. Meaning no tribalism exist at all compare to Kakuma refugee camp, Kenya where fighting happen every day between communities because of tribal communities.

The only problems in Dimma refugee camp was that, No freedom of movement for the lost boy to moved around the community and enjoy the traditional dance either on weekend or any day during the week for that mater. If I made my way into Dimma town to watch traditional dance then coming back to the group would be struggles to get through because of the polices. Every single day of the week the polices always stood by the roadside waiting for anyone from the minor groups coming from Dimma town without a permit to catch them and throw them to jail.

Therefore, in order, to enjoy watching traditional dancing party or look around in Dimma town then you have to get a permission permit from your caretaker, so when you get caught by the polices then you have shown them that piece of paper and they let you go free. I still do not understand why they impose that system of preventing minors to go to town and explore the area.

The only holidays I celebrated in Dimma camp were Christmas, New Year, and 16 May which is the day when the SPLA movement started fighting against Khartoum Government in 1983. During the May 16 celebration, all soldiers dress up in military uniforms together with jerch Amer (the red army) and match on the road for mile and mile singing the military songs. This day was very important to people of Southern Sudan who living in Ethiopia, because South Sudanese people considering this day May 16 as one of the independent day. However, May-16 is not the independent day but the day the SPLA declares the war against the North regime government to become independent nation. The May 16 celebration started in the morning and last the whole day in gathering center field. In early morning it was a parade followed by speeches in the afternoon and then traditional dance in the evening. Food was available so People eat and drink after the officials give speech to the crowds about the condition on front line and the future of the Southern

Sudan. The soccer teams from all across the Dimma camp played games on the day of May 16 miyo.

The South Sudanese celebrated each holiday differently in Dimma camp, Ethiopia.

In Christmas, people always had a great time. It was not like as the Christmas here in the United States of America where people give gifts to each other; Watches television, eat, and drink. In Dimma camp or all other camps I had been to, people do not give gifs because nothing to give and no televisions to watch except just eat and drink. But not every body in Dimma camp always enjoy or had good time on Christmas day especially the lost boys in Minors groups. I remembered when I used to go to the church during the Christmas morning to join the group of other people who are matching on the road singing the Christmas songs of Jesus Christ. I watched youth choir dancing on front of crowds singing joyful songs of Christmas spirit. After the parade was over, we went out to the community to celebrate Christmas by going door to door and ask people for candies. You knock on door and say yiit mabaralekum, Bara wala jua? That mean happy Christmas, welcome in or not welcome in. The owner of the house will say welcome in, she/he either give you candies or money. If no one open the door to welcome you in that meant nothing to give. It is exactly like Halloween here in U.S.A. During Halloween time her in America when no light on no candies or nobody at home. In Dimma camp we do not go door to door when is dark but at daylight.

It was after the military training was over when I was able to go to church on Sunday and some time on Saturdays. Pastor Machar Thon was in charge of the church in Dimma camp during that time when I join the church service. He was the one who baptized me plus the rest of my friends. I remember that day; it was long day service from morning until the sunset. Because there were large number of people who want to get baptize on that the same one Sunday. The Pastor asked me what Christian name I want to be call. I said Peter! I did not even know how I came up with name Peter to be my Christian name, this name Peter just pop up in my head when father Machar Thon asked me on my turn to get baptize. I was not prepared for the Names selection I did not know they will ask me that question.

On New Year and Christmas celebration: There are a parade and traditional dancing afterward. All different tribes in Southern Sudan perform all kinds of culture activities that include dancing as one example of those activities. Everyone dresses up with his/her best clothes for the holiday. At the dancing field, I moved from one dancing group to another to watch them, it was just like changing a channel on television. People eat and drink all kinds of beverages. Holidays in Dimma refugee camp, Ethiopia was the happier time to everybody. People welcome you to their houses for dinner even though you do not know them and they do not know you.

I remember that day when Dr. John Garage de Mabior the SPLA commander together with Salva Kiir Mayardit his assistant commander came to Dimma camp two years latter after the first visited. Salva Kiir was first with some other leaders ridding in a car while Garang was behind with his bodyguards. We knew they were coming to visited us in Dimma camp thus we were waiting for them. That morning when they were, pasting through our group from Marcas to Dr. John's compound everybody was just running toward the vehicles singing the songs of SPLA movement. At first, we thought kiir was Dr. Garang because he came first to the town. Jerch Amer (red army) I am not him the big person is coming, said Salva Kiir.

Of course, no one could hear him in car because of the loud noise from the crowds.

The bodyguards got out of the cars and walked beside the car where Salva was riding in. The refuges in Dimma camp always got excited when one of the SPLA leaders came for a visited and update the people with the news in Southern Sudan.

White beans and maize or maize flour was the only food we had every day on daily bases in a minor group. Some time if you eat too much white beans therefore, you end up with belly pain and a lot of gust. I used to go out in woods with some of my friends AKuot thiawut to get wild green pepper so we could put it in our white beans in order to prevent gusts from occur when eating too much of it.

One thing I hate the most about living in Dimma camp was the force orders from the leaders. They order us the lost boys to go to the bush and get woods materials for their houses. Not just any kind of an order but by force with a rope attaches to your neck meaning, if you do not get those materials you get punish still even you got punish you have to get those materials by any means. They make us go to their homes in the community to build the houses for them. We have to put grass on a roof, mud wall it, and then plastering the mud wall with sand just for free labor.

Some time I wondering maybe that was the reason the put us in a minor group so they can order us to do things for them. The SPLA officials who were in charge of the lost boys some time order us to build our own houses but that is very understandable at all, because it is my house and I have to build it so I could live in it. It would make more cense if they ask for favor to help and with appreciation afterward. However, no pad on back, it would be a miracle to hear word thanks from officials' mouth at that time for whatever we did. They said to me that whatever we make you do is to make you strong and responsible in case you pump into any kind of danger since we are in war, it is our job to teach you survival skills.

At least that is what they said.

"Accept whatever you have been offers for by the helper and make no argument for it is not enough."

CHAPTER 11
Jebel Rhad, South Sudan

In 1991 was the time I fast through Jebel Rhad again for the second time. It was not a great moment at all. It was awful sad moment to me and to all of the refuges of Southern Sudan due to conflict among Ethiopian people. Perhaps, this war affects me very badly in so many ways. Being in a place where I do not really belong does not make me safer and speak freely. I did not know how their government work and the down turn for those who are not happy with government. In fact, that what happened to the country of Ethiopia in 1991 under Mengistu Haile Mariam's power when entrains people started the war against the government of Ethiopia. Entrain did not like how Ethiopia nation moving according to theirs interest so they decided to break out and become independent country. I do not blame them for the lives of a thousand of Southern Sudanese children, women, and men who lost their live in the river of Gilo and Rhade. However, warning would be nice to move out before started the war, since we were refugees and the visitors to that country. I did not things I was blocking their way and it was not my attention to do so. I did not understand why they shot us with the machines' guns. Why they chased us with tanks? Why they shot us in water while we were swimming away for our lives? I am sure I was not shooting back at them but why the Entrain rebels fired rockets at us while we did not even have any weapons on our hands? Maybe it was a set up by Khartoum regime because they are good at buying another rebel groups just to kill us. The Eritrean people would not do this for no any reasons at all and they know we were just campers. Entrain people knows that we were not their enemies and we did not refuse to live the country.

The large good number of Southern Sudanese people, men, women, and children died during that day of Entrains war mostly by guns shot and drowning in the river of Rhade and Gilo. I saw a dozen numbers of people come running for their lives toward the river and jump into the water and disappeared. Even though you know how to swim the fear of shooting guns and out of breath from long run escaping e the danger makes a person not to swim successfully. In addition, over flow of water with strong current was another weakest link to swimming. Where did they go? I said. Under the water, drowning someone stood beside me replied. Oh God! I am so lucky I cross the river before the current wave was not too stronger yet. I thank God as well, said the person beside me. Get down on ground children do not you see bullets flying in air, one of the elders yelling somewhere in woods hiding. I did not say a word when I heard a voice of a person yelling at us to get down; I fall on ground on my belly as soon as I heard him.

Oh! My God some time I wonder how did I past through of that long road I took at age of six without care from parents. The river of Gilo and Rhade took all the lives of my friends and family during the time of exit Ethiopia. I see many people jump in as they are going for a swim but never come up to the surface. Bullets were flying in air like the wild bees. I was so helpless I did not help anybody from drowning in water because I was too little to help anybody and I was scary scared of the strong wave of water going up and down making so many humps and spin so deep all the way down. There was one bulldozer in Jebel Rhad that which one of the SPLA soldier used to put people inside of it and cross them to other side of a river. I was the first one lift by bulldozer to the other side of a river. He made a couple of trips to the other side when he came back for another round the current was getting stronger and stronger so he could not make it. A bulldozer sucks down together with a soldier who was driving it and some few children who were inside of a bulldozer.

It was not an easy journey from Jebel Rhad to Pakook (Koor chum) where I stayed for a year. It was a day journey, water and food available but it took me more than a day to reach to Pakook for some reasons. Perhaps, everybody was in a sorrow mood because of the Entrains attack thus, no one was in mood of walking faster.

Our caretaker Mading Deng and Duach dit were there with us. Duach dit went a head of us and Mading remains behind to make sure no one got lost. It was still dark when I was arrived to that place far way from the town of Pakook. The place we camp in did not even have a name just open field with long grass and trees around it; which later became an airport where the Red Cross agency drops down sorghum by aircraft. Then of course, that morning the elders and women with theirs families went to actually town of Pakook while the minors groups remain at the same camp. The officials made us stay at the camp for a couple of months before they decided to move us west of Pakook town. I had been raining on for the entirely of my staying in the camp. No shelter or any sort kind of hut roof to sit in and stay dry from rain. I used a plastic sheet to cover myself with when it was raining. I did not mind or care of the water coming below as long my body is cover from the top. "At that moment the water coming from above was the priority to prevent and a flood was the mystery."

CHAPTER 12
Pakok camp

The SPLA officials decided to moved my group again to Pakook town from the airport and they made me waited there while they were on a search for a new place to relocate my group. This place was an open field without grass on ground but with few trees around it. During the daytime, I stay under those trees and sleep in an open field at night. A plastic sheet was everything I need to live with, the bed, mattress, and hut. When the weather is clear, I lay down that plastic sheet on ground as my mattress and sleep on it and when is raining I used it as a shelter.

It rains nonstop most of the time in Pakok. Some time I do not even bother to put a plastic sheet on me because it's torn apart and it's not doing any good. I used my heavy blanket instead to cover up in rain. When a blanket-got sock with water, I keep breathing in and out through my mouth into my body under a blanket. My big brother Ring taught me that theory. "The air that coming out of you will keep your body warm said my brother Ring."

Month after month was gone by while still waiting for the news of the new location to reside. They move my group gain for the second time out of town a little far west of Pakook. This place was all grass and trees everywhere perhaps it was bush without any open ground what so ever. We sleep on grass under the trees. We probably spend some good weeks in this place. Then they move us again to a place where we actually started to build our own shelters. It was call Pakook minor group of Dimma. In all these four places, we been moved to, we were in the same groups as we were in Dimma camp in Ethiopia the Dik dik group, Marekrek group, and Jesh Athuot group. The three groups always sat separate, each group sits under a tree of their choice as one family.

Seeking for a safety shelter never came to an ended to me during those days of my traveling across to the neighboring countries looking for a safer shelter to settle and "catch my breath from a long run away from danger than I thought it would be." When Eritrean liberation force (EPLF) and Ethiopia government started fighting against themselves in 1991, it forced my fellow's Sudanese people and I out of Ethiopia back to Pakook in Southern Sudan. I automatically knew in my mind that the journey started over again from the beginning just like when I left home of Kalthok.

However, due to lack of food the life in Pakook camp, South Sudan was formidable to resist for so many months I spend there before I head to Kakuma refugee camp, Kenya. The life in Pakook was worst than the life on the way from Kalthok to Ethiopia in 1988. All through my journey to safety of Ethiopia, I always moved from place to place and hoping that in next stops, I might get something to eat meanwhile, in pakook I was staying in the same one place for a long time without food, or clean water. Perhaps, the only things I used for food in Pakook camp were the wild fruits such as Kuech, Abuuk, and Dhong. The leaves of the sweet potatoes and the leaves of the cassava plants were also food I depend on.

The Ugandan people owners of the garden harvest all every thing and left only leaves and unwanted cassava and sweet potatoes. I ate the fruits of Dhong tree, which I never tried before in my life. It does not have that bad of taste, just no flavor to it; taste like mud. When I was at home of Kalthok, I saw people use this Dhong tree to put on grave. Indeed, Dinka people use it as the flowers to bring with them when visited some dead family member in cemetery so they can place it on grave of that dead person. So for me to imagining this theory of Dhong tree, made me so afraid and not want me to touch it, but I had no choice but to eat it in order to survive. It was the only tree with the most fruits to eat in the area. In fact, the hunger was driving my soul however; it left me no choice to stay away from it. I picked them up and boiled them for a couple of minutes or two then eat them. As side effect, I got dizzy with a headache, a heavy belly-offset mood.

Pakook is a small town located a couple of miles South of Jebel Rhad border of Southern Sudan and Ethiopia and in west of Ponchalla. Pakook was occupying by the SPLA troops meaning no civilians except some of the Ugandan refuges were only civilians living in Pakook, when I got there. These Ugandans people were rebels who break out of Uganda, moved to Pakook to hide themselves, and redeem their power I guess. The SPLA government allowed them to enter to Southern Sudan because they were no harm to the people of Southern Sudan.

They weren't under (UNHCR) United Nation High commission for Refuge's care; they were protecting and ruling themselves under secret government of their own.

Therefore, we called them refuges but they called themselves freedom rebel fighters as their identity. They feed themselves by cultivating all kinds of fruits and vegetables such as sweet potatoes, cassava, sorghums, papaya, and groundnuts.

Most of them moved along with us when we left Pakook camp to Kakuma camp in Kenya in 1992.

The Ugandan people save my life and the lives of the other lost boys of Southern Sudan who were living in Pakook camp as well with the work of their hands. The garden of cassava, groundnuts, sweet potatoes, maize, papaya, and sorghum that the Ugandan planted sure did help me from starving to death. Cultivation was the only way this Ugandan depend on otherwise they would have nothing to survive because there was no the UN to provide them with food.

Of course, they were nice to me thus; they gave me food when I asked for it.

However, at the end I disappointed the Ugandan people by destroying theirs food garden with my own hands in disrespectful way. Stealing their plants and robbing them was not nice, but they did not blame me for that, they understand my situation. I realize afterward what I did was wrong, robbing Ugandan's gardens of groundnuts, sweet potatoes, and cassava was not appreciative at all. I was not myself those days in Pakook camp; my head was not functioning the way it supposes to work, it was staring by the hungry spiritual minds.

I remembered those mornings when I used to wake up very supper early in the morning to go to Ugandan's garden to get just some potatoes leaves and cassava leaves so I could boil and eat it. I was in a desperate situation of food; I do not care about how bad that food is. I eat it any way and not worry whether I am going to die of poison or not.

The SPLA government put us into groups in order for them to be able to manage such a large number of lost boys in a group. The people in each group were like family. They looked out for each other, and lived together and shared all the responsibilities. My group that was Dik dik group had three zones: zone one, zone two, and zone three. However, these three zones are breaking into three groups:

Group one, group two, and group three. All of the subgroups are break down into another three small subgroup: First subgroup, second subgroup, and third subgroup. Each subgroup contains twenty-five or more people base on the number of people in-groups. The group is lead by Jauech and subgroup is lead by Arip follow by Wukil.

After they relocated me to a final permanent place where I resettle for some duration of time, I started to build shelter to live in while waited to move onto new place. I knew that Pakok was n't a place where they want refuges to stay because it was n't safe to live there. However, for the time being, each group has to build one big hut for group to live in. The work is dividing among the three subgroup and each subgroup is responsible for certain types of items they need to get. It is Jauech's duty to make sure the job has to be finished as soon as possible. So by doing that Jauech has to give orders to Arip and Wukil and then Arip give orders to Wukil and Wukil give orders to a group. This system of grouping was how we count and take care of ourselves since In Dimma camp in Ethiopia and it never stops until we came to USA. Each group and subgroup has to know who is not feeling well today and all groups have to provide some soup and comfort him then bring a sick person to the doctors. In fact, teamwork and care of one another was what make us alive until today.

Some bad things happened in Pakook camp, thing that jeopardizes the life of human being. On that evening of the day I do not even remember, I was there when one of the Marekrek person died from undiagnosed disease. I watch him struggling for his life on floor kicking and role over screaming on top of his lungs because he had stomach pain. Mother Azor dit plus two of the other women doctors from Red Cross agency Joanna and Mule were there on that evening when his friends and group mates brought him down to a clinic. His stomach was full of blood therefore, the blood came out of his mouth, nose, and honest. The doctors tried to give him some kind of medications to bring him back unfortunate it did not bring him back. I was frightened to see something like that and made me worried that this disease might affect everybody. The doctors belief that could be some kind of microorganism disease he might have drink with water because of the dirty water we had been drinking since the day we got to Pakook camp. From that day, mother Azor dit announces to all the minor groups to boil any water for drinking before drinking them.

My caretaker Mading Deng almost commits suicide in his house across from Dik Dik groups' gathering field. One night he locks himself inside of his house with loading gun tried to kill him over unfair jail time by the one of the SPLA leader. He was sent to jail for something he was not aware of doing. No one wanted to explain why he was send to jail and without a lawyer to follow his case and defend him. That offset him very much and made him think of killing himself.

Good things his brother was there standing by the door talking to him not to take his life. I was there too and everyone from my group was there standing a couple feet away from the house. We didn't say any thing to him we decided to let the brother do the talking because they know themselves very well and they understand each another. Thanks God he did not end up doing it. It took him long time holding his ground and finally he did listen to his brother's voice.

A week later after the incidental of my caretaker's problem, one of the SPLA commander came to Minors group in the middle of night and gather all Matothot/the adults minors with rifles. He orders them to drop theirs guns on ground for no reason whatsoever. Mading was there too that night he refuses to put his gun on ground because he was caution about commander's plans. The commander was going to shoot everyone after they unarm and because of my caretaker Mading's disagreements with the idea of lowing guns save, lives that night. The commander was really going to kill everyone in the groups and that was the reason he gathered the adults men first because they men have guns. He was going to joint the rebels to fight against the SPLA Government. After a couple of months settled in Pakook camp, the SPLA government decided to distributed guns to the adult men so they can go and hunt for food and feed the young minors like me who does not have strength to carry guns. There was nothing else to eat except to go and hunt for food in wood on my own. That night none of the Dikdik groups were not there at the meeting because we were sleeping and we did not have guns so the commander didn't bother getting us up for the meeting.

I did not know about the meeting conducted by Commander, until I heard about it from my caretaker the following morning.

This person was one of the SPLA commanders selected by the officials to look after the lost boys. He was in charge of all the lost boys, or in the another name (Jesh Al Amer)/ Red arm in

Dimma camp, Ethiopia, so very much everybody in minor groups knew him who he was. People were shock to hear what he tried to do to Jesh Al Amer, the people he was taking care. From that day, I never saw or hear from him at all. I do not know where he went or what happens to him. I think he runs away on that the same night of the incident I am not sure. At least that was his plan anyway. He wanted to defect from the Government after he killed large number of people especially the lost boys.

A month after I arrived to Pakook camp from Ethiopia and another one more life was gone. It was around eight o-clocks in the morning when they started urging over the radio. The radio was belonging to Akoi; he brought it with him from Ethiopia to Pakook camp at the time of exiting out of Dimma camp, Ethiopia because of the war that breakout in a country. Akoi was the head caretaker of all the minor groups and Atem was in charge of all the South Sudanese refuges since Ethiopia until Pakook. I guess Atem orders Akoi to give his radio to Atem and Akoi refuse to do so. Atem was not asking Akoi in nice way but by force and Akoi did not like that idea. They yell at each other back and forth for some couple good hours until Akoi got offset, he took a gun out, shot Mr. Atem in head, and then shot himself in head too twice. They were both rush to Pakook hospital for medical attention, however, Akoi did not make it he died right there in Pakook hospital while Atem was transfer to lokichogio hospital in Kenya by Red Cross where he got better care then from that day I never heard how Atem situation was in Lokichogio hospital. This incident occurred inside a small hut in the middle of Pakook town near Ugandan refuges compound. The people who were there outside listing to their argument tell the story to everyone in town of what exactly happened. My friend Biar told me everything about what actually happened between akoi and Atem. Biar is relating to Akoi he was even call over to come and stay with Akoi in hospitals. That how I know what exactly the root caused of death.

I did not know where the South Sudan government got the herd of cows. Since there was not anything else to used for food in Pakook camp. They used these cows as my food supply in Pakook camp. One morning I was outside under a tree thinking of what to do for the day. As I lift up my head, then I saw many cows coming from nowhere pasting by grassing a long slowly to a cattle camp where they had been kept. I was surprise to see many cows in Pakook; I thought those cows were belonging to Murlei tribe. The government of South Sudan always thinks head of time of what to feed the refuges if the UN does not get there on time. Our Government decided to followed us with cows to depend on for milk and meat after I moved out of Ethiopia. Who knows where did they get the cows? They are the Government who cares where they got them. The SPLA Government appointed Mr. Salaman to be in charge of all the cattle. It was his duty to picks out some of the adult men to joint his teams so they can look after the herds and take care of them by milking and leash them down on post. Since these cows were the only source of survival at that time of residence in Pakook, it was Mr. Salaman's responsibility to select some healthy cows every four weeks to be slaughter for meat; the SPLA officials gave him orders to do so. These cows indeed did play a big role of saving my life and all the other lost boys in general during those days of hardship in Pakook camp. We benefit from those cattle in two ways: dairy milk and beef. The SPLA official leaders together with Mr.

Salaman set up a schedule days in a week where every group have a chance to get some gallons of milk on that day of the week. Then perhaps, the milk has to go around by turn among three groups of the lost boys that were break down according to ages which were jesh athuot (Adults), Meeker (young Adults), and dikdik (young children) group. Even though there were no enough gallons of milk for everyone to fulfill theirs need, it was better than nothing at all. The waiting period was two weeks or more and those two weeks were like forever because those gallons of milk were the only food I depend on. When it was Dikdik group turns to receive milk, each person ends up with one cup of whole milk. I do not drink my one cup of milk right away at once after I receive them; I used them as soup to dip in sorghum wungali and save the remainder milk for the next day.

Refrigeration was not important issue to me in Pakook camp. Nowhere to get a refrigerator in Pakook for that matter because no big, small business or any business shops at all for that mater to sell stuffs like that in pakook. "In addition, even though you do have it for some reasons which I doubt no one ever has one, then no power to plug it in so to work." I did not have that kind of money to buy something like that and even if I had money, I would spend on buying food. I never worried of my milk going bad because it never last to get raw, beside, I will still drink them even though they get raw to the point they become cut cheese.

Some long weeks waiting for my group turn to come so I can get milk and the hunger tried to drag me down to hell. "Hunger ties the rope to my neck and makes me feel hopeless and weakest; hunger was the danger parasite that ate me a live from inside during those days in Pakook camp in June of 1991 until 1992." The number of sick people from the actual diseases was not large at all than the number of people who were affected by the hunger. "Even if you feel sick, the doctor can't tell what you were really sick for except hunger"? In order to be able to survive in Pakook camp, I have to be active If I don't get up supper early in the morning to go to Ugandans' garden for some Cassava leaves and sweet Potato leaves to boil them (remove) and eat then I am in bad luck to fast the day. I remember one day I was in front of our hut laying down on floor side ways with my legs and knees bend all the way to the end of my chine. I look around while I was laying down, I saw some of the children from my group sitting, and some were laying down in front of the huts and some under the trees not sleeping but just zoning because they are very weakening by the hunger. Under those trees and in front of our huts, we were like a fish in a pond without water, jumping up and down with a mouth open thirsty for water and in need of food. A throat dried up and stomach was nothing but an empty host and just like a balloon without an air, which make it difficult most of the time for me to go to the woods and find wild fruits to eat. But still a group leader orders people to go into the woods to walk around and look for the wild fruits to snack on instead of people to just staying in one place laying down to sleep. You could go by yourself to the frost to find something to eat, if you have energy to walk that far even though a group leader did not say so. Also, when a group leader saw a situation like that then he had to reported the condition to our caretaker Mr. Mading Deng and Mading could talk to Mr. Salaman to shorten a waiting period and provide healthy cows to be slaughtered for food early before the scheduled week dateline. Every day, day or night our caretaker Mading Deng always goes around in the groups, hut by hut checking people to be sure no one is dying inside the room. He looks at everybody to see who is very weak from hunger or sickness and then he has to report to Mother Azordit that was our doctor and mother at the same time in clinic to be watching carefully.

Mr. Salaman does not past by that more often to cattle camp; maybe couple of times after week and half of the last day of distribution of food. He snicks by some time through quietly without anyone spots him otherwise he be asked when is the next slaughter going to happen. My group was on the road to cattle camp whoever past through there I should always know unless it was at night when everyone a felt sleep. Whenever we saw Mr. Salaman on his way to cattle camp, we always called him Buo as his nickname. Everybody came up with that nickname, as a sign of yes or no from Mr. Salaman's responds about if today is the lucky day to get beef. If we call him Buo and he says it back Buo jesh al amer/red army then I know there will be food today but if he did not reply then nothing is going to happen on that day. I always feel very sad and down for native response from the food suppler because it is going to be difficult a long week to wait for food.

Mr. Salaman had to make sure there were enough cows to be slaughtering for every minor groups in the camp, did dik, adult group of Jech Al thout, and Marekrek group. Mr. Salaman divided cows among both group accordingly to the number of people in each group. I remembered my Dik dik group always got three cows for that length of two weeks. You would not belief how bad people were dying to get food to eat in Pakook camp, South Sudan. Some part of a cow's part remove end up in my stomach while a cow even still standing up. As soon, we I receive our three cows from cattle camp on the day of contribution. Each person in Dik dik group wanted cow's tail to roast and eat before the meat is ready. Cow's tail was the only part that was easy to get. Every body was anxious to have something in stomach right away at that moment. I tried to find my way closer to a cow without anyone seeing me and cut off cow's tail with a knife. At that moment I have cow's tail in my hands then I rush to where a fire available to roast it. Course everyone made himself a little knife out of metal cans to dig the ground for a buuk fruits in wild. That was how badly I starving in Paycheck camp.

However, even the cows I killed in Pakook camp in those days of drought understood why we took their lives. I did not take these animals' lives in curl way but to save my life from starving to death. At least nothing wasted in whole cow parts, I consumed every thing I mean every thing that has included skin except the bad product inside an intestine of a cow bone.

Three cows for my group, each zone has to have one cow to eat and managed it to last four weeks period. It was zone leaders' responsibility to make sure that the meat is spending wisely in order to last longer until next slaughtering day.

The meat always cook in one place in a big barrel then distrusted to the people of a dik dik group, each person end up with a couple pieces of meat. When we got cows for our zone, we skin it and then put skin, legs, and head in a save place that will be the last dinner after everything was gone. We let the skin rotten and then we clean off the hair of it, we put it in a barrel together with legs and head to cook for approximately of whole day from morning until evening time.

The SPLA government never gives up to kept all the lost boys alive in general.

They tried their best to provide food to keep everyone staying foot when no UN agency around. Even though it did not satisfy every body's need, no one blames the government for shortage of food and clean water in Pakook camp. During those hard times in Pakok camp, it forced some of the lost boys to escape to Ponychalla and to Buma. Some of the people were killed by Anyuak rebels on the way to Ponychalla to searching for food. Moreover, on the way to Buma some were attack by wild animals. The South Sudanese refuges from Pinyudu where settle in Ponychalla. However, the refuges from Dimma were in Pakook camp that was after the war broke out in Ethiopia between Eritrean and Ethiopia government in 1991. The refugees in Ponychalla camp, South Sudan had little food supply drops down by plan. The food was provided by UNICEF agency. The refugees in Pakok camp heard what was going in Ponychalla camp that was food available. Therefore, some people decided to go to Ponychalla to get food but pakook chairperson Mr. Malong did not want anybody to leave the town because of the Anyuak rebels' situation on the way to Ponychalla. Most of the people escape anyway, some did not make it to Ponychalla and some did. Nothing was going in Buma but most people wanted to go anyway for sake of the new environment experiences.

Before the plan drop off the food in Ponychalla camp, the SPLA troops in Nyat base contributed some maize corn for just the minor groups in Pakok camp.

Therefore, Mr. Malong selected some few strong men and sent them to go and get maize corns that had been provide by the soldiers in Nyat. It was a week journey to Nyat so it took these men longer to get back with food sooner, because they were weak from starvation. In fact, most of the maize corns were very much gone because the people who went and got them spend some of the corns on the way back to pakook camp because they were hunger and nothing else for them to eat. They were give orders not to touch that maize but they did not have choice not to do so, in order for them to be able to walk, they ate some of the food. Turn out those maize corns were bad, no body really knew where that food supply originated. The maize corns were nothing but some kid of chemicals all over them. When I put them in a pot of water to cook however, they turn water yellow and they taste bitter. I eat them anyway because nothing else available to depend on except these bad maize corns so not to think more but to just go a head and risk our lives. I didn't care what will happen next but may be that why I did not get poison from these maize corns because I wasn't worried to die so my God almighty blesses the maize corn to save my life and not got sick.

Finally, the food arrived after the long months of waiting on Mollie and Jennifer survey about the refugees' life situation in Pakook camp. Jennifer and Mollie were Red Cross agency workers. I belief they were sent to pakook camp by UN officials from headquarter in lokichoggio, Kenya to observe my condition and get reports back to the agency about the refugees situation. However, the UN was able to sent plans to drop the food off in pakook camp, South Sudan. The airport was that place where the SPLA officials made me settle in when I came to Pakook from Jebel Rhad border after I departure from Ethiopia. This place was where the Red Cross agency used as airport to drop off the food. First day of food drop was the happier moment of my life. Now I have enough food to eat. When the plans started dropping off sorghum, some of the bags broke therefore, sorghums spill everywhere on ground. Of Course the airport was not hard floor concrete; it was all sand ground, however, the sorghum all mix up with sand. None of the sorghum in sand did not go waste at all, I collected them and separated sorghum out of sand. I never did a good job separating sand out of Sorghum completely.

Some of the sorghums were still mix up with sand. However, that did not stop me from eating that sorghum though. I put them in a pot and boil them and then I eat them. Most of the dirt sunk underneath the pot but little tiny rocks blend in together with sorghum.

I did not know where my next move was going to be. I knew on my mind that Pakok refugee camp was not the last safe place for all the refuges to staying.

There were been rumors going on about moving out of Pakook camp since I got there but nobody knew when and where to? Perhaps, most of the lost boys could not stand life in Pakook camp in 1991 until 1992 therefore, as results of that, people escape to Buma and then to Kapoeta tried to find better place to live and get food. The SPLA officials always return people back to Pakook camp when they caught escaper on the way because theirs concept was for the lost boys to stay together.

It was time for place change; I said it in whispering inside voice to a person standing next to me on that morning when the refuges from ponychalla camp pasting by in a big crowds group. The lost boys from Pakok camp line up standing besides the road-saying hello greeting to south Sudanese brothers and sisters who were on move out of Ponychalla camp to Kamuma refuge camp, Kenya. I end up going with them eventually latterly that week. I asked them where they were going but they did not even know where to either. I thought might be they were joining me in pakook camp to stay there but they kept going exiting the area next morning. Most of them spend night in pakook camp on that day and some of them just kept going straight to Nyat town near Buma. At that moment,

I thought I was not ever going to move along with them because the SPLA leaders who were in charge of me in Pakook camp. They did not say anything about moving all these times I have been in Pakook camp. Suddenly two days latter the SPLA officials told me to pack my stuffs and followed a long the other groups of refuges to Nyat. "When I heard the word we are all moving along with them," I was so static indeed, because I was thirsty of getting out of Pakook camp. I didn't care where to but as long I was moving out of Pakook camp was okay with me, whatever ahead will be mystery. I believed in nomadic theory because I always feel energetic and realest when I am on move to new place. I do not worry about the bumps along the way to where I am going and may be that why I always break it through.

I spend three days on the way to Nyat; it was not too bad of a journey just very slow move without a fear of enemies except the fear of the wild animals such as loin, hyenas, and wild cats. However, it was not the big issue to worry about this problem because there were not that many wild animals around during that time of season; may be few of the animals attempted attack from now and then in swamp areas along the path. The refugees from Ponychalla camp and refugees from Pakook camp became one group along the way. We identify ourselves as red arm of Pakook and red arm of Ponychalla even when we were in Kakuma,

Kenya.

"No much of medical equipments and medications available, no good healthcare building to admitted very sick patients in Pakok refugee camp but with a touch of motherhood, it was all good. Mother Azordit was there with the refugees especially the lost boys. Everybody in minor group called her mother. Indeed, she was a mother, a father, and a Doctor to all the lost boys of South Sudan in Pakok camp. When I had problems, I always go and talk to her. Her words of advice toward my sorrow always make me feel myself again."

CHAPTER 13

Nyat

After I arrived to Nyat, the SPLA Government let me stay there for some months which I did not even know exactly how many months I spend in Nyat. Nyat was very small town where only the SPLA armies occupied to patrol the town and the other towns around that was including Buma town. It was hard to live there due to lack of water, insecurity, and food shortage. So much large number of refugees in that very small area make it more difficult to find water. Fetching for water was a challenge condition because of the distance of water location and the fear of killing by rebels. Therefore, the soldiers had to scout me to the river to get water however, people have to go in large group and some soldiers a head of line for protection from rebels attack. That was the first day we got to Nyat but after couple of days, the SPLA Government decided to deployed some troops a long the river to stay there for the whole day and come back to town at sun set when no one of the civilians in the area. That is mean everyone has to get water before the sun set otherwise no water for the night. Some of the Murlei people were in Dimma camp, Ethiopia as refuges until Pakook but when we came to Nyat they disappeared, they all went to theirs villages because Nyat was one of their home town.

CHAPTER 14
Boma

I have no an idea why the SPLA government did not want me to enter to Boma at day light. It was nighttime when I got to Boma may be it was just me. Most of the other groups arrived to the town of Boma ahead of me at daylight. I arrived there at night and I left while it was still dark to Khor chuei/ the street of tamarind. I think the whole concept was, the SPLA officials did not want young minors to explore the area because one might like it and get an idea of escaping from the group and stay in Boma. However, Even though you get a chance to escape, the governor of Boma will find you and return you to your minor group leader Mr.

Deng Makeny. I did not get to look around to see how the Boma look like; I heard about it when I was in Pakook camp and I was looking forward to explored and see inside but did not happen, as I want. On that night of my way through, I stop in Boma town for quick eye shot nap before proceedings on our journey.

Perhaps, the life in Boma was harder to live too due to lack of food, people of Boma were depending on cattle for food to survive just like when I was in Pakook camp but no enough beef for everybody. Thus, the chairman let the beef cooked in one place and then distributed to people. I guess that night of my present he goes around the group of people sleeping in open field in town asking people to go to his compound for juai diak/ small bowl of soup. Then one person did not understand the message because he was a little bit sleepy. This person saw a commander going around talking to people and the people wake up and walk to the compound so he followed those people to the compound as well.

Nevertheless, the chairman saw him going in and he did not remember telling that person to go for Juai diak/ small bowl of soup. However, the town leader stops him by the door and asks him where he was going? Should you be waiting for your turns to come? Boss, I heard you telling people to go to your compound for Juai diak and I did not get the message so I am going for Juai diak too sir he said. "The chairman laughs and said you will survive if you sleep with one eye open, go in for Juai diak son."

I did not know what happen over night and I was not aware of the story until the next morning when some people who knew about the story escalated it to the public. "I guess I did not sleep with my one eye open that night therefore, I missed going for Juai Dinka/ the small blow of soup." The story of Juai Diak by chairman of Boma town and Deng Makeny's story about wrong answers to the interviewer due to lack of understanding of English language in Pakook camp were the stories we used to tell ourselves as a joke so to make our day when we are in sorrow mood as we always been. Deng Makeny was one of the caretakers in Pakook; he interviewed by one of the Red Cross agency worker bout lives in Pakook refuge camp. Some of the questions asked in interview by Jennifer to Deng Makeny were as followed: are these children soldiers? Do they have parents? How long did they have been without food? Are they carrying guns? Do they have clothes, blankets, and mosquito net? These are all the questions Jennifer asked Deny Makeny but due to misunderstanding of English question therefore, Deng's answers to all these questions was yes. I Am sure Jennifer was aware of all the interview situations as limited English language so she did n't really take it seriously. However, after Janna left, some kids from the minor group who knows English approach Deny and tell him that, Deny you answer yes to all the question asked by Jennifer but most of them are not correct: like the one question she asked you, are all these children soldiers? The other one she asked you if we are carrying guns. I did say yes to all the these questions! Asked Deny Makeny! Yes, you did, said the kids. Thus, Deny run after Jennifer yelling Hey, hey Jennifer, all those questions are No! Suddenly Jennifer turn around and say, I know Deny and just smile as she toward her bike cycle. Then everybody started laughing as soon Deny started running after Jennifer yelling. From that day, the story started so every time when we see Deng Makeny pasting by we always make joke about him for his answers to the questions and his reaction afterward.

"Hey, hello Jennifer all the answers before are all No." he never get mad about the joke and for making funny of him, instead he joints in and laugh with us.

CHAPTER 15

Khor Cuei (Street of tamarind)

It was just few more stop on the way to street of tamarind to rest and I was there in town. It did not take me much longer to reach to the town of street of Tamarind on that morning day. I was very tired and sleepy when I got to town therefore, I crush under a tree shad that was in middle of town. It was daylight so while I was under that tree I was thinking of finding my way to were every body of my group is sitting latter on after I rest. Of cause street of Tamarind town was another place without civilians but only the SPLA soldiers. It was the maximum of two days resettlement but I went through the same process of protection from known roaming rebels in bush to get water in river as like exactly in Nyat camp.

Perhaps it was a distance away to where the river was, however, no one allowed to go to the river alone and after the sun set, no movement. No body knows why the Murile rebels were in mood of just killing. I was just pasting through by theirs villages with respect toward them and their properties; perhaps I was afraid of them. Moreover, none of us did something bad to one of them. I guess they were just playing the game of do not care, robbing and killing was the only picture appeared on their faces. Next morning some group head the road to Sahara of Kothngor where every body staying for some days under the SPLA Government protection from Tapotha rebels looting. Then days latter, my group followed a long as well to Sahara of Kothngor. I do not remember how long it took me to get there but I know it was long journey indeed to that place called Sarah of Kothngor.

CHAPTER 16
Sarah of Kothngor

This was another refuge camp in middle of nowhere, only very few of the SPLA soldiers occupied the area. The tribe around Sahara of Kothngor was Tapotha tribe and they have some young gang rebels among them who actually attacked the camp more than one since I had been resting there from the beginning. The Tapothan women came with some meat of any kind such as sheep and goat's meat to sale to us with blanket, mosquito net, and bed sheet. What weird about this was that I never saw Tapothan men came with these mention items above to sale but just women. It makes me wonder why only the Tapothan women were the only one come to the camp to sale meat and not men. May be it is something to do with culture where men do not do such kind of job. We did not trust Tapothan people meat product that they were sale to us therefore, I decided not to except the actually dead meat from them but only the life goat or sheep.

Because some of them sale dog meat to the travelers most of the time. Perhaps, you cannot tell dog meat from the other animals after being skin. The water situation in Kothngor was the same as just in Nyat and street of tamarin; but worst than that. There was no river with real actually water; it was dry swamp with very few wet spots spread out in distance from one another. However, people have to dig the ground to get muddy water under the ground. Since there were no water treatment tablet and water filters to purify that muddy dirty water. I treated those dirty waters on my own. I put muddy water in container and let it sit there for some minutes for dirt to sink underneath. Alternatively, if I am thirsty and needed water in urgent, which was the exact condition I was in anyway. I took a root of Ameyok plant and chew it first before I drink water then drink water; it makes muddy dirty water taste sweet. Ameyok is a type of plant that has seeds and it does grow in moderate areas. The Ameyok seeds are bitter and they are dangerous to eat without proper procedure method of make it eatable. Back home in Kalthok in South Sudan, my mother used to collect Ameyok to feed us with it during the food shortage. She goes to where the Ameyok grow to get the seeds then spread them out in sun to dry for days. After drying process, she puts the seeds in basket that made out of leaves of a palm tree then place them in water for some days in order for bitter to fate away in by water. After that, she cooks the seeds and ready to eat. Only the God knows what was I drink with those water during that time in Sahara of Kothngor camping. I was waiting for Red Cross agency in Sarah of kothngor camp to come and scouting me to Magoth town. It was a dangerous path through to Magoth because of the Taposan gang rebels. These groups were monitoring my move since from street of Tamarind to Sarah of Kothngor. Day after day facing toward the road looking for Red Cross agency flag on vehicle to appear but no sign of it at all until that one-day morning when I woke up and saw a dozen of Red Cross big trucks standing in line cover with plastic sheet. Inside of these trucks were food, maize and beans with cooking oil. The Red Cross workers and SPLA officials started contributing food to every one in camp. Each group end up with good amount of food that day therefore, the whole life situation regardless of what to eat was good but fear of insecurity was the biggest problem. Sahara of Kothngor was a large camp with many people all under the trees and long grasses and only the SPLA government was our hope of protection, which indeed was through out of our journeys seeking for safety. This place wasn't like the actually Sahara where there's no any tree or grass what so ever, its got some trees and grasses just like other bushes. I used these long grasses for shade during daylight, which did not do much for shading, but better than nothing at all. The rebel's eyes were on refuges, however, it was critical to attempt pasting through to Magoth therefore; the Red Cross agency used delivery trucks to bring the refuges to Magoth. The Red Cross small car leads the way with Red Cross flag flying on aerial as always. Thank God the did not attack us on the way to magoth until later during the week after we arrived to Magoth.

CHAPTER 17
Magoth

Not even a day and one life was taken away by the gang rebels group and not just one but many lives. This was another attack I was lucky to be a live. He was so young just a kid, and now the rebels kill him for no reason. I do not understand why the gang rebel groups Kill Thon Mabior. He was just a refuge like me without weapons to fight back or attempt to harm any of these rebels, now he left his little brother behind without any one to look after him. I remembered him; he was in my group, the Dik Dik group since Dimma camp, Ethiopia until pakook camp, South Sudan. It was day two in Magoth when the gang rebels attacked the camp, just to loot people with food, clothes, blanket, and to killed people. There were only very few of the SPLA armies guarding the camp but the number of people in camp were big therefore; soldiers did not guard half of the camp. Every night was a nightmare past through it to the next morning. Everybody in a camp wishing for daylight to appear sooner which made no much of the different either because the rebels shoot people even at daylight, but to see the sun coming out was a release. The rebels always forced their way into the camp in dark and do what they wish to do, all unnecessary things a person with pity can't do to other human being such as kidnaping, robbing, and killing. Even during the daylight, they would not leave us a lone. They climb on trees and shoot us down under the trees from above, that we were lodging at the time. I thing the rebels were training themselves on us we the refuges how to aim their target right on foes. In fact, I was not theirs enemies but brother from the same country, South Sudan. I did not understand why they want to kill me. Even you can hear them laughing loud in woods after they shot someone dead. So it was fun for them to kill other human being. I do not know why the Taposa attacked me when I was not in sense of hurting them. That was the question no body can provide good explanation answer even taposa tribe themselves.

I waited for three weeks in Magoth for Red Cross to come back with food from lokichoggio in Kenya the humanitarian aid head quarter. The Red Cross left afterward when they brought the refuges from Sahara of Kothngor to Magoth.

These three weeks were like a year because of the rebels disturbing; it was so painful to stay there at that moment. Now the Red Cross arrived with more delivery Lorries full of food however, security situation was getting a bit under control by the SPLA Government. After long days of frightening by the gang rebels, the SPLA commander in charge of Magoth sent alert message to the leaders for increasing of troops to protect civilians from roaming arm rebels.

Every body thought the Red cross agency will lift all the refuges from Magoth to Kapoeta but it turn out there weren't enough delivery Lorries or conveys to lift every body at once to Kapeota. SPLA officials and Red Cross agency didn't want to leave some few refuges in Magoth otherwise the rebels will finish them all.

The UN did not want to drove these conveys to Lokichoggio empty neither therefore, the Red Cross took only sick people. Those who could not walk far or faster because of wounds underneath their feet or with any other medical health issues were the only one lift by car to Nairuse by Red Cross. This when I decided not to walked on foot to Kapoeta because my feet were hurt of long walked since from Pakook camp to Sahara of Kothngor. However, I was stealthily in lorries with other sick people, the caretakers lash me with sticks tried to get me off a lorry but I didn't give up until I made it inside. One of the caretakers tried to get into a convey in order to grabbed me and pull me out of the convey but one of the Red Cross workers stop him not to do that, he is already inside leave him said the Red Cross's organizer. It was around eight A.M when they loaded lorries up with sick people then we departure from Magoth at ten O'clock in the morning. Of course, it was bumping ride because of the poor road through Khor Kelany, Kapoeta, and up to Nairus. It was a safe ride whole the way to our destination, no rebels attack but we saw them running along side of the lorry. Most importantly they did not shoot at us or attempt to aim at the vehicles to shoot.

CHAPTER 18
Kapoeta

It was only one hours to Kapoeta from Magoth. We stopped at Kapoeta hospital for quick emergency respond to one of the sick person among us. It did not take long for UN to take care of the situation even I did not get out of the vehicles. In fact, that sick person remained in Kapoeta hospital for treatment and he was watch very closely by doctors. I heard about Kapoeta since I was in Pakook camp that it is a beautiful place and it got many Mango trees all round the town. I was so looking forward to explore and get familiar with it but unfortunately that did not happen, as I want it. I thought of staying there in Kapeota town for a while. However, I realized even though I remained in Kapoeta town to fulfill my wish of exploring the area and waited for the other group to come from Magoth, I would not have a place to stay because I did not know anybody there in Kapoeta.

Kapoeta has Mangoes tree everywhere but dangerous though to roam under these mango trees because Taposan rebels lingering around and shoot people.
Kapoeta was not like other places I had been to because of the population of people living there, it more mixture of civilians and the SPLA military forces.

Kapoeta is a developed city, therefore, the north government very much knows about it. However, the North Government airdrop booms like a rain drop every single day of the week. Perhaps, people who were living there especially civilians didn't have any other places to go to because by then the Ethiopian Government wasn't longer accepting refuges and the Government of Southern Sudan had no-good relationship with Kenyan government so no one was allowed to enter to Kenya soil. According to people of Kapoeta, every one had to dig a trench to hide when they heard the sound of jet fighter or other war plant. It was obvious the jet can come any time in blinks of an eye without knowing is coming. Everybody had to sharpen his/her ears listen to the suspicious sound of war plane. There was no airport for plane to land so whenever people hear plane noise they automatically know it's danger.

I heard of the stories from some of my group mates about what occurred on their way when they departure from Magoth to Kapoeta. They left Magoth at six o'clock in the evening of the same day I left by car. The gang rebels just ambushed them half way to Khor Kelany, between Magoth and this small town called Khor kelany. Mr. Biet Wol was the head caretaker of the red army (jesh al mer), so he was leading the crowds with some few of SPLA soldiers behind him and rest at the end of line. There were dry grasses along the path side therefore the rebels light grass on fire to see so people coming and then shoot them. At that moment Mr. Biet, spot a fire burning a head so he told crowds to get on ground and be quiet. He went toward the fire with soldiers to clear the way. The rebels saw them coming and the rebels open fire at the soldiers at that moment the soldiers fire back at the rebels therefore, the rebels moved back farther from the path. After that the refuges waited for couple more minutes to make sure the rebels are not coming back to attack. The refuges reached khor Kelany early morning before the sun raise. According to Simon Gai the one who told me the story said that Koor kelany was full of rocks and it was hard to walk around without shoes which in fact very much at that moment no one had foot cover such as shoes or other kind of foot wear. For me when I past through I saw rocks everywhere. It was bumpy but I did not actually step down to feel it on my feet because I was in Red Cross lorry.

Simon said too that when they reached kapoeta they didn't had enough food to eat whatever little food they had was gone with in a day after they reached Kapoeta. There was not UN food supply store in Kapoeta and people of Kapoeta had no enough food of their own to help the refuges. In addition, Simon said that there were so many criminals who roam at night and robbing people with belonging such as food, clothes, blankets, mosquito net, and whatever valuable. I never experienced all the above situations because I did not spent night in Kapoeta but I faced some of the conditions in Nairus. I was in situation of fear by rebels, criminals were robbing lack of food, and water but the only thing absent at night like what happened to my fellow friends who left behind in Kapoeta.

After the refuges arrived from Magoth to Kapoeta then the Red Cross decided not to let them walked again from Kapoeta to Nairus because it was dangerous path through there to Nairus. Rebels occupied that road however, Red Cross had to provide conveys to lift all the refuges to Nairus in-group with high heavy security. Due to large number of refuges, it took Red Cross some good weeks to transport all people to Nairus from Kapoeta.

CHAPTER 19

Nairus

Nairus was a small town surrounded by Taposa tribe which actually their hometown. Nairus is very close to lokichoggio, Kenya. Perhaps, it is considered as boarder of South Sudan and Kenya. There are other small military bases in between and they are security checkpoint. The south Sudan government knew that we are coming to Nairus therefore, the officials called meeting with Taposa community leaders so they can talk to the youth that are in gang groups to make sure no harm to the refuges otherwise there will be consequences. The meeting between two-side does make a different even though there were some few minor problems such as robbery and beating it was normal.

When I was arrived to Nairus by lorry that day, they drop me off near the Nairus clinic so that for people who were sick can get treatment right away. There were three water bore in Nairus which used by Taposan people and the few of SPLA troops who were deployed there in Nairus. Food was shortage, side of insecurity was not horrible, and water available, however, Taposan always come with meat of any animal kind such as life goat, sheep chicken, sorghum, and corn to exchanged it with clothes, mosquito nets, or blanket. There were three of us in group because when I sneak into a convey in Magoth, Puol Nyeth was a patience transported to Nairus the same day I was by Red Cross and I knew him my Dik dik group. Another person of our group was Awur Akech; he left from Pakook camp before us to Kapoeta so when he heard that we coming he went to Nairus to wait there. However, Awur Akech, Puol Ngeth, and I were one group so we make contribution of clothes to food from Taposan people.

It is very hard for Taposa people to kill a cow for food unless they really have to, they are just like Dinka people because people Dinka people adore cow so much.

Taposa tribe of South Sudan and Turkana tribe of Kenya had cow-raiding problem between themselves. this had been going on for quit some time, where by Taposa go to Turkana land and raid cows and the Turkana do the same thing too they go to Taposa land and get back their cows and it just go back and forth between them.

Four weeks latter the convey started appear with some more refuges, day after day more pouring in until arrived to Nairus then they told us to go back to our own group which we were belong since Pakook so that to receive food contributed by the Red Cross agency.

In Nairus, there were two set of refuge camps site and not very far apart from one another. The refugees from Dimma camp, Ethiopia were identify as refugees of Pakook camp and the refugees from Panyundu camp, Ethiopia were consider as refugees of Ponychalla camp, South Sudan. This was how we differentiate ourselves accordingly base on the refugee camps in Ethiopia we were in and then to South Sudan. Therefore, it was Jesh al mer/red army of Pakook and Jesh Al Amer of Ponychalla because the refuges from Pakook camp knew themselves as well as the refuges from Ponychalla. The minor groups always put separate from community groups by the South Sudan officials people in charge of refuges in order for UN to see them and provide school buildings closer to their residential area that was how it had been since Ethiopia camps.

When I was back to my old group, the officials moved my group to a new location far away from middle of Nairus town toward the direction of Kapeota.

The SPLA officials resided women with their families there in town. It had always been like that when my group comes to any new place, families in town and minor groups outside of town. Maybe they really do not care about me that much so they put my group ahead as the shield, at least that was the question everyone in minor groups asked every time once in new area; even when I was on a journey, they let me go first.

No body knew where next therefore, our caretakers made us build some huts to dwell while waited for the green light from the Kenyan Government. I heard the rumors about going to Kenya but I did not know for sure when will that happen.

However, each group of ten members had to build a hut. My group of ten members was break down into two groups. Some went to get grass for roofing and the rest went to the frost after materials such as tree branches to used for main poles and ceiling grates on the house.

Due to large number of group of refuges and with a little bit of food available in Nairus camp, made the Red Cross agency decided to gave responsibilities of food management to group caretakers. Perhaps, food was shortage at that moment.

Of cause as I mention it already above, whatever available was not enough for everybody in a group. Our caretaker was not really taking good care of the people in the group particularly in Nairus base. He enriches himself with food that given to a group by Red Cross so caretakers could manage it well to feed everyone with it. Instead, he used that food supply to buy himself some goats and sheep from Taposan people. Everybody in group wasn't happy with him because of mistreatment so one night during super time, one person from the group throw some heavy rock into the caretakers' compound and strike wrong person which didn't attempts to be a victim Mr. Geng Maker. He was nice to Jech Al Amer and he had no any problem with anybody in the group whatsoever, may be that is why the rock hit him because of his generosity. The person who throws the rock was targeting the head caretaker unfortunate that's did not happen the way jesh al Amer wanted. Two minutes after the incident the whistles scream, it was the head caretaker responsible for whistle blowing. He felt the hated from the group then he called the meeting aggressively, going around the groups lashing people with tree branches want people to come to parade. After everybody gathered, the first thing came out of Caretaker's mouth was that:

"Whoever responsible for rock flying into the compound to step forward. As he said it then everybody in a group step forward together." That night he got the message, he learned that people are not happy with the way food is spent. Then from that day, he changed a bit. I respect him always as my leader and not just only the leader but also as an adult. It is Dinka, s culture that you should respect any person older than you.

No body was aware of the attack will occur in town of Kapoeta. It was quite normal morning day therefore, some of my group members and I went into the woods to get materials for our hut. We did not go far in bush away from the group camp. It was around 6 o-clocks A.M when I left group for materials searching. After two hours, which was eight o-clocks and the whistle, scream in the group camp, warning people to stop whatever they were doing and come back to the group campsite. As soon I heard the whistle, I drop every thing I had in my hands and I run to the group. When I heard the whistle blowing, I knew something was wrong. The caretakers taught us we the minors a certain way to be able to know the sound of whistle, whether it's blow in normal way or in way of danger warning. Normal way will be single peeping one after another in couple second apart this is just for gathering to give information or to go some where for mission. However, rapidly whistle blowing continually indicated that there is danger. Whenever you hear this sound of a wired screaming whistle, you immediately come to gathering field immediately. That was exactly what happened that day in Nurse Refugee camp. The warning sound of whistle blowing save me from being lift behind alone in wood on that day in Nairus camp. When I came back to the camp, everybody was gone. I was so afraid;

Therefore, I did not get all my belonging out of storage location, which was under a tree where the group was lodging. "The only thing I grab was my sleeping blanket that's it." I saw groups of people come running out of breath from Kapoeta, very much all children and women. They remain behind in Kapoeta hospital for medical attention. When I heard the whistle I did not know what was going on, I just knew Something was wrong. When I saw these people who were coming from Kapoeta town, I asked one of them to know what was going on.

Then he told me that Kapoeta town is under attack by North Sudan forces. He added! The foe came unexpected this morning and shelling the town, who knows what damage they did to the town and the people!

It was very rough journey, a lot of looting and killing happened that day in Nairuse when I rushed away for my life toward Kenya for safety. The tribe of Taposa of Nairuse town and outside of Nairuse got involve robbing people with food and clothes on the way. It was horrible unorganized journey I ever been to.

Good numbers of children were run over and kill by the crowds. The Red Cross agency food storage was destroyed. Everybody was afraid that there would be no food in Lockichoggio. However, everybody wanted to have food for the next stop if she/he made a life there. For me it was too late to get food out of the Red Cross' food supply storage. It was already gone when I got there. It was as like no storage had been built there at all. In fact, getting food was not in my mind at that moment but get out of Nairuse alive was my biggest concern.

It took me day and half to reached lockichoggio Kenya where I stayed for some months, which I do not even, remember how long. I was so tired and did not want to walk anymore, but I did force myself until I reached the resting area. I do not even remember what happened on the way to Lockichoggio or how the road was like. Most the Journey was at night and it was dark to see anything at all. In delight it was the sun was so hot and which made me not think of any else but to stay in shade. The only thing I remember was seeing the lights on mountain in distant. It was Kenya security base on mountain. In my mind I thought that where I was going to stay. I walked for some hours hoping to get to that light sooner but never come close to the point of reach. After couple of hours walking a car drove pasting by to pick up sick people behind, they told me the place is just a minute; therefore, I walked faster so I can sit down and get some water. I was not to the stopping area in a minute like the driver saying. He was lying, he just wanted me to get excited and move faster. It was a slow journey without resting at all, no one wanted to sit down for a break because everyone thought that the enemy was following us. I did not get to Lickichoggio until the next day.

CHAPTER 20

Lokichogio

When I was arrived to Lokichogio refugee camp, the UNICEF agency workers where standing beside the road with water jars on their hands to gave to the people. They hold water in your mouth to drink and they pull water out of your mouth if you tried to drink too much. They tried to avoid people getting sick in stomach from drinking too much water with empty stomach. I did not go too far to where I was supposed to be. I fast out right there beside the road where the UNCIF workers hand out water. They did not bother me when I laid down there; they let latter brought me to where everybody was sleeping. Next morning I woke up and did not know where was. There were no civilians living in Lokichogio at the time I was arrived. Only Turkana tribe was living there but the police do not allow them to enter into town. Therefore, they were living far away from Lokichogio town. I do not know why. In addition, I did not think of asking someone about it because I got my own problems that Ii have to worry. I did not have anything to eat for like two weeks to three weeks. I was carrying nothing at all except my blanket from Nairuse to Lokichogio Kenya. It was because I missed the time when people broken into the Red cross-store food supply. Good thing though, some of my group friends got some rice they brought with them from Nairuse and they share with me so I was not that starving bad.

Due to urgency, escaping from Nairuse because of the enemy attacked in town of Kapoeta. People crash randomly under any tree a person can find near by. It was hard for some people to find where they were supposed to be which was their group location is. However, it took long time for UNICEF agency figure out how to distribute food to people in groups because of that problem. The only thing the UNICEF had it available and does not need group to get certain mount was water.

The UNICEF agency brought water somewhere by water tangs and I do not know where, they poured those water in barrels and everybody needs water come and get some water for drink or showed. Getting water was not easy though, you have to get up very early in the morning to water otherwise, and you get no water for some days. There were very few water tang trucks and because of the long distance to where the water resource located, it took drivers many hours to come back and turn around next trip. Therefore, there was not enough water every time for every one in the camp. Some people will get water today and some do not the same as the next day. That was also because of people population in Lokichogio Kenya camp.

It took me a week to find my group's location. All these seven days out of my group, I was sharing rice with some of my group mates whom I met in the same place I was sleeping that night. They did help me a lot to survive otherwise I would have been in bad shape for these seven days without food to eat.

Even after I jointed my group, another week was gone without food supply from UNICEF Agency. However, I did not just sit down to wait for UNICEF to provide food. Instead, I went into the forest to find wild fruits to eat. I gathered any thing that I can find such as wild berries and leaves of certain plant. I boil the leaves and then eat it. I went out every day, seven days a week in wood looking for something better to eat. Nothing else to do at the camp but to just stay in one spot for whole day which made it very hard to fast the day. I never stopped going to hunted for anything that eatable in order to keep me holds on while still waiting for the UNICEF agency to supply the really food. Going in wood was not safe neither because of the Turkana people. They always wanted to kill anyone they came across in wood. Therefore, the one safe way was to go in groups than one or two. The Turkana would not attempt to attack unless they are more in number. Most of them always had guns. However, do not talk to them or even say hello when you fasting them. They always look mad and I do not know why. No incident shooting happened in lokichogio camp by Turkana only more rapping and beaten occurred every single day. There was no security scout protecting the camp but each group was responsible for the safety of people in-group. Once in while may be at mid night the Kenyan police car run through the groups just to scared Turkana rebels away if they tried to attempt to attack the camp.

Everybody finally found a group where he/she belong and that was exactly what the UNICEF wanted to see before the food was given out to people. Now the agency is willing to supply food by group according to number of people in-group.

At first, it was all rice, beans and vegetable oil. After couple of months, it changes to maize. My group received twenty sack of maize for total of one thousand people or more. It was not enough for everybody in-group but better than nothing.

I never bothered of building huts in Lokichogio camp because no body sure that was going to be a place to live for while. The UN distributed some plastic sheet to people in order to use for desired effect of rain. Every new place I went to: under a tree was always my shelter so I when camp to Lokichogio camp I found myself a nice tree with a lot of shade. This tree was everything I needed to live on, the rain blocker and the sun blocker. Since it was super hot during daylight, I stayed under this tree for cold shad. I never moved an inch away from that tree since I got there until I came to Kakuma refugee camp.

There was no school to go to in the morning, you woke up and wonder what to do for the day if you do not feel like going in wood today. Since I was in Dimma,

Ethiopia and all the places I had been, word of God was my second school. I used to go to church every day. I was in Sunday school singing groups. When I was in Lokichoigio camp I went to a church every day to learn songs and dancing technique. Many of the lost boys were attending church every day, seven days a week. Due to large number of people who wanted to learn church songs and dancing technique but there were very few teachers available, they break the groups of Sunday school down into small groups so each group can come according to schedule time. I was scheduled to come in at eight o-clocks AM to noon. This was very a productive program indeed, I learned many songs all about praising God. Some time they let Sunday school groups perform dancing activity in front of congregations on Sunday service.

The people in the church played a big role in my life in Lokichoigio Kenya. They save me couple time from hunger when I did not have anything to eat. Father pastor Machar Thon at the time he lets the women prepared some meal for me and other Sunday school children and called us over to his compound to eat.

Going to church on those days indeed kept me out of trouble and loneliness otherwise, I did not know what direction I would end up to?

It was obvious in my mind that Lokichogio was not the finally refugees home.

Every single refugee was aware of that. I knew I am going to Kenya and not back to South Sudan. However, I didn't know to where in Kenya am I going to stay All the South Sudanese refugees were afraid of going to Kenya because they think Kenya people will kill us all. After the UNICEF agency announced to everybody in the camp that we going to Kakuma refugee camp no body wanted to go first for the purpose of untruthful of Kenyans people. People thought that the Kenyan would hand over the refugees from South Sudan to Arab north; at least that what people thought after what happened in Kapoeta.

Mr. Ajang Alak was the chairman of the refugees at that time. He came up with his own idea to let people go to Kakuma refugee camp accordingly by tribal group and it works. After first group arrived to Kakuma refugee camp and not heard of any harm from Kenyan people then every body realized that nothing dangerous about going to Kakuma after all. From Lokichogio to Kakuma was long way to walk. It might take couple of days to reach there. However, the Red Cross agency lift people by conveys to Kakuma, one group at a time. It took a long time for UNCHR to lift all the groups to Kakuma camp because there were many groups and many people were contain in a group to be transport to Kakuma.

CHAPTER 21

"Kenya."
Kakuma refugee camp

I came to Kakuma refugee camp on July 17/1992; that was the day the UNHCR decided to load me up on lorry and brought me to Kakuma refugee camp, Kenya.

It was long ride indeed from Lockichoiggio to Kakuma. I was standing up throughout the entirely time all the way to Kakuma because there was no open spot to sit due to luck of space on back of a lorry. I do not know if the UN was considering how many people were suppose to be on back of a lorry. There were total of 45 or more of us on back of a lorry. All squeeze together like cows being transported to different place.

I was in-group two minor in zone one. Group 3 and group one minors were already brought to Kakuma camp before my group. The UNHCR place them in zone one. Everybody in my group was sleeping in one big open dry land. The other groups were doing the same as well. There were no shelters built when I got to Kakuma camp. The part of camp that the UN resided my group and all the other refugee groups was totally in forest area. There were thorn trees everywhere. On the other side of my group was one Turkana family living in two huts that were build out of cow dung. I was afraid to go near them because of the UN and caretakers' advices. They told me not to play around with Turkana people or not even go near them they might get aggressive and tried to harm you. I was new to them of course and they were new to me. May be they did not like the idea of refugees being resided on their land. I can tell the reaction on their faces the way they look at me in the camp. "They even say it loud and clear in my face, go back to wherever you came from." they did not know the meaning of being a refugee; they thought we are coming to dominated their land. I do not know if Kenyan Government told his people that are include Turkana people about my purpose of being in their country. May be to some of them but not to entirely country otherwise for some who did n't like the idea of refugees being resided in Kenya would have protesting not to bring refugees to their country. Might be they already protested when I was still in Lockichoiggio. That I do not know. May be that was one of the reasons it took so long to come to Kakuma camp.

The bathroom situation was nightmare in minor groups; however, sanitation was very poor indeed. In fact, diarrhea out break happened every day because of that. I was one of the victims affected by diarrhea out break. This diarrhea was not like normal watery diarrhea but a bloody one. Of course, there was no hospital or local clinic to go to in Kakuma camp before then. Instead, I treated myself by drinking mixture of salt and sugar together with water. It helps me from getting dehydration. Perhaps, there were no doctors available to go to at the time.

The UNCHR built temporally bathroom for all the minor groups of zone one, zone two, zone three, and zone four to used for time being. The UN officials themselves and leaders of the camp did not wanted people to go in wood for bathroom. They were afraid that Turkana will attack anyone goes outside for bathroom. Beside, It did not take long for those temporally bathrooms to get dirty. No one ever thought of cleaning them at all for that mater. As the result, people end up going to the bathroom in wood. The Turkana people attempt couple of attack in every group across the camp.

After couple of months in Kakuma refugee camp, the Turkanans population increase. Some of the Turkana people who where living far away from the town started to move closer to where the refugees were located. They UNHCR even hired very much most the turkana people to drive trucks to groups and drop off food. Some of them were in charge of loading food into trucks and brought it to distribution centers around the camp. Most of the security gate watchers in UNHCR compound were Turkanas. So coming of refugees to Kakuma was not a bad idea after all. It benefited Kenyan in many ways and the Turkana realize afterward that the refugees brought jobs to the area. Kenyan shops were busy:

Sudanese traders were buying goods from them. Business buses owners profit was over split because a lot of Sudanese, Ugandans, Somalians, Ethiopians, and Burundians refugees where traveling every day from Kakuma camp to Nairobi or to any other part of Kenya for business or other important things. The economic of Kenya became increase and more productive all because of the Refugees in Kakuma.

Life was good for Kenyans people and bad for me because I was a refugee. I was living in fear of Turkana killing and lack of enough food plus other need such as medical care. Food situation was bad indeed. For fourteen days, my ration was 7kg of maize corns, rice or wheat flour, ½ liter of vegetable oil, and One cup of bush beans or split peas. Some time fourteen days exceeded to another week without food. I did not know where the UNHCR get all the food. However, in my mind I assumed that the UN has more food supply to distribute to people everyday. I did not know the UN have to ask international community and donors to feed me. In kakuma camp, some time I blame Kenyan workers who were in the UN compound for food delay because I thought they want me to starve and that they decided not to give food out to people according to timetable when fourteen days end.

Every distribution day always, a challenge to everybody in camp because one distribution food center for one zone and for the large number of people was totally nightmare. After fourteen days everyone in the camp got nothing left to eat so, the people waited anxiously for distribution day to come. Most people spend night in distribution center to be the first one on line so in order to receive his/her ration and have something to eat on that day. In my minor group, we help one another by owe food to someone who did not receive his ration on that the same day so we could all have something together on that day.

So many lives were lost in Kakuma refugee camp from Turkana robbery and tribal violence. Turkanan were having guns therefore, Turkana were not afraid to show up at any time in their target locations such as shops and inside the groups. None of the refugees had guns to fight back at Turakana robberies. Perhaps, UNHCR was our protection shield. The UN talked with Kenyan police department in Kakuma so they could go around the camp for look out every night. However, these number of polices could not be in every group in one night at the same time. There were many groups of refugees in Kakuma; a thousand of them may be I should say but I am not sure the exact number of groups all together that were in Kakuma refugee camp. I know there were three camps in Kakuma that were form by the UNHCR in order to accommodate all the refugees. Kakuma one,

Kakuma 2, and Kakuma 3 both were full of refugees. Kakuma one refugee camp contains five zones and in each zone, there were certain number of groups. I do not know exactly the number of groups in each zone but I do know the number of lost boys' minor groups in each zone. The minor groups were always separated from the community groups every time I moved to a new refugee camp. This community groups were people with their families and all the relatives. The UNHCR and caretakers from SPLA government built schools in minor groups in each zone and the kids from the community attended school there. There were five minor groups in zone one in kakuma one which where five of the schools were built in each of them. Group one, group two, group three, group four, and group five were In Kakuma one zone one. Group two minor was my group. The minor groups' caretakers, teachers, and SPLA representatives decided to name all the schools in Kakuma camp accordingly base on the name of towns and cities in South Sudan.

However, the names of schools in zone one were as followed:

School of group one minor: Jebel Mara primary school.
School of group two minor: Barelnaam primary school.
School of group three minor: Nimule primary school.
School of group four minor: Pochoda primary school.
School of group five: Rajaf primary school.
Schools of zone two were:
Juba primary school.
Kaduuguli primary school.

Sobat primary school.
Imatong primary school.
Schools of zone three were:
Shambe primary shool.
Nile primary school.
Torit primary school.
Aweil primary school.
Rajah primary school.
Schools of zone four were as followed:
Boma primary school.
Wau primary school.
Malakal primary school.
Kush primary school.

There were no lost boys' minor group in zone five, therefore the UNCHR did not put any school in that zone. All the children from zone five went to school in all these primary school that were built in each lost boys minor groups in zone one.

Not until later the UNHCR built unity primary school in zone five in order to reduced the population in each school in zone one.

Three of the secondary schools were built in Kakuma refugee camp and one Technical school, which was Don Bosco. Catholic missionaries built this technical school. In fact, Don Bosco School played a big role in Kakuma refugee camp.

Especially among the young men like myself who didn't get the chance to go to secondary school because I did not fulfil the requirement grades point average for secondary admission. Most of the people who did not get good grade or past KCPE always join Don Bosco technical School. And that where I went after I set for KCPE exam and did not past. My electrical career started at Don Bosco technical school in Kakuma refugee camp. I got my electrical certificate the year before I started the process of coming to USA.

Two of the secondary schools were built in zone three and one of them in zone one. In order to go to secondary school after finished grade eight and after KCPE, the Kenya national exam, you have to get the maximum of 350 or more grade point averages. That was the exception number that school administration had set as the pasting grade to go to secondary school; otherwise you have to repeated grade eight primary school if you want until you past the maximum pasting grade of 350 point in KCPE national exam or you could just joint Don Bosco technical school.

Kakuma 2 was very much occupied by Somalian Bantus refugees; and Kakuma 3 was the mixture of Somalian Bantus and some of the south Sudan refugees who came later to Kakuma.

The children from these two camps went to school in zone two, zone three and zone four primary schools because these three zones were not far apart from Kakuma 2 and Kakuma three camps. The UNHCR later built one school in Kukama three camps just for kidgraden graders because the little children could not travel that far to go to school in the other zones.

I always went to bed without depression or stress after listening to stories. Telling ourselves stories and jokes before bed every night in Kakuma camp was the only medication to my depression and stress. We used to stay up telling stories until mid night. Getting together and laugh was the only way we cheer ourselves up and not thinking a lot about home and family. Very good number of lost boys got seriously sick and die because of that and some had mental problem. Some were thinking too much about home and parents and how they could go back and find the family members but there was no way out to do that because nobody even knew where to start searching? Therefore, the depression and stress become out of control. However, without good doctor to go to for therapy and medication, it always results to death.

It did not take too long for UNCHR to built schools in Kakuma refugee camp after everybody arrival to kakuma. However, it took long time to built shelters for people to dwell in. It was because the UNHCR was give out materials to built shelter accordingly just the way people arrived to Kakuma camp. Meaning, the first group entered to Kakuma had to receive building materials first. At first, the UN provided everybody with plastic sheet to use for rain and shad purposes at moment. My group two minor was not near of getting materials any some time soon. I did not know how long I waited for building materials to arrive to my group. I knew it was long enough because my plastic sheet the one UN provided me torn apart. The UNCHR distributed wood poles and palm leaves for roofing.

That was the second thing they gave out to people after plastic sheet.

In every time of food distribution cycle, the UNCHR had been saving empty oil cans so people could used them as iron sheet for roofing. They gave people living in the same room one hundred empty oil cans to make form of iron sheet out of them, by just cut it open and connected them together. I used nails to secure the can iron sheet onto the roof. The UNCHR gave out certain amount of cans for your house however, if you get more than enough oil cans for your house then you have to sell the rest for money. But if I do not have enough cans to finish cover my entire house rooftop, then it is my responsibility to buy more cans from other people who had more cans in order to complete covering the roof of my house. I had some money in my pocket during that time of construction because I decided to size down my house into small hut however; I end up with more empty cans left over so I sold these cans for money to other people in need of them.

After I came to Kakuma refugee camp, in couple of months later the UNCHR took a picture of me. They let me hold up a 12"*12" black board against my chest with my name written on it. I did not know what was the purpose of the picture taken? because I did not asked and nobody told me about it. It was not just me, whose was photographed; the UNCHR took pictures of all the other lost boys in minor groups around the camp.

When the process of coming to America began, I realize the reason why they took my picture in first place. "Even then, I still don't know who made the process of lost boys from South Sudan to come to America happened?" It all started when few names of the lost boys appear on board for an interview in UNCHR compound in the morning. They said it was just a first trial to see and figure out the way to make interview process more easy and simple. It was only very few number of people from each minor groups. I saw the lost boys going to the UNHCR compound every morning. They have to be there for 8 o-clock in the morning for an interview.

The second list of the lost boys going for an interview were displayed on information board but my name were not on that list. At first before the INS involves the UNHCR hand out the names of minors in each group-to-group's caretaker to make sure everybody's names were on list. The screening of names for everyone in-group was the first thing UNHCR did in order to speed up the process. Another thing the UNHCR did after names screening was taking photo ID of every lost boys in groups. They used the same systems of taking photograph that the UNHCR used the day I came to Kakuma refugee camp; the system of holding up 12"*12" blackboard against the chest with my names written on it.

After my photo ID was taken, the UNHCR worker placed my ration card paper, photo ID, and my life story together in one file.

It was JVA agency turn to take over for interview process. My name was not in the first list, second or the third list neither but in fourth list my name appeared.

During all these time of waiting for my name to come out for interview, I never stopped waking up every day in the morning to go and check for my name on information board. It was a moment of exciting when I heard that the American government accepted the lost boys of South Sudan to resided in USA. I could not believe at first that the US was going to bring all 26,000 lost boys to America.

Even though some of the lost boys did not come to America for some other reasons, at least most good number of lost boys made it to USA.

The interview was conduct in three different steps. The first step of was names screening, organized by lost boys' group caretakers and UNHCR workers and that was done in Napata secondary school in zone three. Joint voluntary agency (JVA) main interview office was in UNHCR compound. JVA agency was very much interviewing people base on person's life story background. They asked me where my parents were and if I heard from them. My answer to these questions was: I do not know where my parents are. I never heard from them for a long time. I am not sure if they are all still alive or dead. I did not speak good English back then so the UNHCR hired my group caretakers to translate. Therefore, all my responds to any question was asked by an interviewer then I answered the questions in Dinka language. The JVA interviewer asked me why I want to come to America? I said to be safe and started a new life without the fear of guns and killing. I added more answers to the question: I told him that I want to go to bed and sleep through the whole night without worried of enemy attack at night and to go to school. The interviewer just kept his head in paper writing something down. I do not know what he was putting down in that paper? The only time he looks me in eye is when he asked me question. I was told by the caretaker who was translated me not to look down but to look in eye of interviewer so he doesn't think you are telling lies. According to Dinka, culture when a kid is talking to an adult he/she is not supposed to look person in eye. It is the way of showing respect to a person bigger than you. Since it was already in mind not to look in person bigger than you his/her eyes, I did look down couple of times during my interview. A caretaker who was translated me explains the situation to a JVA agency interviewer. I guess they all understand the situation and that was not a big concern they looking for to fail you.

Second part of resettlement process is done and they told me that I got couple more steps to go and INS as one of the next steps that take place after JVA.

Twinecarf was the head quarter place for INS where they did interview. My name came out right away for interview with INS a week later after I was done with JVA agency. It was 15-mile walk from where I live to Twinecarf. It was whole day process from 7:00 AM to 5:00 PM at evening hour. The INS person asked me how old I was and I told him that I do not know my really birthday. "You don't know your birthday! He said it in surprise voice." I said yes I do not know my birthday because we do not celebrate birthdays and for me being away for quite so long since I was little. I do not really remember anything about my birthday accept the sound of guns that caused me to leaving my home. He did not say anything after that. He put his head down and started writing something I did not know what was it that he was writing down on paper. Since I did not give him my birthday, he went a head and gave me my own birthday, which I discovered later when I received my approval letter to come to America. The INS interviewer asked me if I would ever come back to South Sudan some day. I said yes I would love to come back some day when there is peace in the country and reunited with my family if they are still a live. After he asks me the last question, he stood up, shakes my hand, and he said good luck to you Peter! I did not say nothing back to him I just shake his hand too and walk out of the room. I worried that I was going to fail the interview.

Most of the lost boys who went for an interview first before me started to receive their approval or denial letters from department of INS. From that day of my last interview with INS, the only place I had to go to check for my interview result was the UNHCR compound. School was not in my mind any more at that moment because I knew and hopping that if I come to America, education will be better, safe, and interesting. However, I woke up every morning and head to UNHCR compound to wait for my letter. It took me more plus steps back and forth from compound to my group until that day when I receive my approval letter to come to America. It was ten miles walking on foot everyday for quiet some time but it was worth it after I got the letter. January of 2001 was the month of my happiness. In fact, on 01/10/2001 was the time I received my approval letter from INS to resided in the United States of America.

Even after I got approval letter from INS to resettle in America, still there was one more requirement step left for me to fulfill. A medical exam was the only way to determined whether I am, allowed or not to come to America base on my medical results. On Oct/11/200, the IOM called me for medical exam to IOM mobile clinic center in Kakuma refugee camp. There was a long line of other lost boys waited to go in for physical on that day. I did not get up early that day to be the first one on line so I was far at the end of line. It was long day waiting to get in and see the doctor. When it was my turn, the nurse called my name and walked me to doctor's office. She brought me in and told me to sit down on chair and wait for a doctor to come in and see me. I was so scared that I am going to fail medical exam because I never went to the doctor for a long time for physical check up. I never had a doctor in my whole life. In fact, I didn't know what disease I had and which I don't and that was my biggest fear of all. When the doctor came in, he asked me what part of my body is hurting. I didn't respond to that question. He asked me again sir where in your body is hurting the most all the time? I still didn't have answer for the Doctor. The doctors said, peter, do you want me to get down on my knees for you to tell me about your health history? I said no doctor, my chest and my back are hurting sir. He said, that was not hard to open your mouth and say something is it Peter? I was shy but not only that, I couldn't understand the doctor's American accent. He pulled out chest x-ray and he places it on reading light. The nurse took my x-ray the day before my physical exams. He looked at it and said your x-ray look normal to me so nothing wrong with your chest and your back. He took out his Stethoscope and he listen to my chest and my back your breathing is just find, he said. The doctor put back Stethoscope around his neck, he reached his hand to shake my hands and said good luck Peter it's nice to meet you today. I said thank you doctor I hope to see you on the other side sire. I did not know if he understand what I said because of my English?

From that day after my medical exam, I didn't know if I past medical exam or not.

I was just waiting for my name to appear on information board to fly to USA.

Another sign of hope to come to America just happened after couple of months waiting for green light.

On third of March 2001, my name came out for orientation. IOM agent conducted the orientation. In fact, the IOM was in charge of transportation and medical exam for all the lost boys who were coming to United States.

When I saw my name on board for orientation, I knew in my mind that I past medical exam. I was so happy that they didn't found any disease that will avoid me from coming to America.

I was informed by the IOM trainee to come with only paper and pencil to orientation tomorrow at 7 AM in the morning. It was eight hours class, from 7 Am to 3 PM. I couldn't' wait to be in class because I was anxious to learn more about the life in America. The IOM trainee person didn't tell me everything but just only the basic information they want me to know. There were many of the lost boys wanted to do orientation but very few number of trainees available. Therefore, orientation time was shorten. The first thing he talked about was under age girls rules in America. To have sex with under age girl is a crime in America and you can end up in jail or face deportation to a country you belong, said the IOM trainee. I knew the reason he started class with this topic, he was aware where I came from that there is no law like that exist in my country. I guess sex with under age girl was the most importance information they want me to know first before the rest of the topics. They didn't want to run out of time without being able to say something about under age girl rules in America.

The more topics followed on the next day. Now the IOM trainee is going to talk about job. He said that In America everybody has to work for living and finding job is a challenge to refugees like you. The trainee lay out the importance steps of finding job in America. The IOM trainee person mention that if you going for a job interview, you need to dress up appropriately. This will impress the employer and know that you are responsible person. Never look down when you are being interview by the employer; you have to look person in eyes. If you look down, he/she thinks you are lying.

"Law in America is applying to every citizen, so it does not mater whether you are refugee the law will charge you like other American citizens the trainee said."

He talked about rent too. In America there's something called landlord. This word landlord mean property owner. People pay money to this person so they can live in the house. The owner of the house, which is landlord, always makes sure that person want to live in his/her house got good record. Therefore, he/she has to do some background check in order to find out weather you are a good tenant or not. So in America good credit is always more valuable indeed. However, to keep your high credit score up then you have to pay you bills on time otherwise the next landlord you want to move to will not allowed you to rent his/her apartment to you he said.

He also mention about sales tax in America that when you are purchasing something in store or elsewhere. You have to be more prepared with enough money in your pocket because everything you buy there is always sales tax included. Therefore, to have extra money in your pocket will avoid embracement of not having enough money to cover the cost of that item you are getting.

I thought sales tax will be the last topic but I was wrong. He kept going with more important stuffs that I was not even interested of knowing. Look at someone for too long, Spitting in public places, and touching other people were the topics that he talked about after sales tax. In America, it is rude to star at someone for quite some time. Its make a person uncomfortable and it can cause conflict between you and that person. Quick look is not a big problem only continually straight staring at someone is the issue, he said.

Touching other people without their awareness is not a good thing in America. If you bump into someone accidentally then you have to say sorry or excuse me.

Then he/she knows that you did mean doing that intentionally.

When I came back the next day, I thought he was going to talk about more stuffs.

However, I didn't know that was the last day of orientation.

Good morning class he said. Today is the last day of your orientation and you are going to receive a certificate of completion of welcome to the United States of America A guidebook for refugees' orientation. The IOM trainee person walks into orientation class and he said, congratulation and good luck to you all, he said. Anybody with a question, he asked the class. I saw five to seven hands up among some of the lost boys who want to asked question. I wanted to raise my hand to asked question about driving in America but I decided not to raise my hands. I was hoping that one of the five lost boys who raised their hands at least one of them will asked that question. Perhaps my hope came true. Driving was the first question asked by the first pick person. Moreover, the trainee's answer to driving question was when you are in America you definitely need to have driving license to move around especially going to work or school. It all depends on a person interest. Some people choose to use public transportation for some reasons. Perhaps, one of these reasons is money saving or not want to drive at all. To own a car in America is very expensive because there are many requirement stuffs to it, insurance as one of those stuffs. Every car has to be insured for protection purpose. Car inspection every year is require on every car to make sure is in good condition to be on road. Vehicle registration is a law in America and every year you have to pay money toward registration renewable requirement. To drive a car to work or to school every day is require money for fuel.

There are some steps toward getting driving license in America: first is to get driving permit then the actual driving license. Gaining driving permit does not means you can drive a car on your own, you need someone with a license to guide you otherwise, you can get in trouble with the law, the trainee said.

After he finished talking he didn't allowed another questions to be ask because of the time. He was holding certificates in his hand. He puts his head down on paper and raises his head back up again with my certificate on his right hand. He called my name and I went in front to receive my certificate. I guess he puts the names in alphabetical order. Therefore, my orientation classes about life In America end on March 10/2001.

On May/09/2001 two months later after the orientation was completed. My name appeared on information board to leave for America. I was so excited; I could not wait to get on an airplane. That would be my first time ever to fly on an airplane. I didn't do much though to prepare myself for the journey like going to store and buy some clothes and shoes to wear on the way. Besides, I didn't have money anyway to buy clothes or shoes. Most of the lost boys did buy more clothes and shoes because they had money and they wanted to spend before they leave for America. Some decided to give their money out to some friends or group mates who were remained in camp.

At the orientation, the IOM person told me not to worry about buying more clothes or shoes but just some pairs of clothes and shoes for the road until I got to my destination.

I left Kakuma refugee camp on 5/09/2001 at 10 O-cock in the morning to Nairobi Kenya. The UNHCR took me inside the compound to hand in my ration card before I left. It was the requirements set by the UNHCR and the chairman of the refugee camp Mr. Deng Dau that if you are leaving the camp for resettlement then you have to give your ration card to UN in order to keep track of the number of the lost boys leaving for resettlement. After I handed in my ration card, I waited inside the UN compound for and airplane to arrived from Nairobi. The departure time from Kakuma refugee camp to Nairobi, Kenya was always at 10

O-clock in the morning. When it was time to go the UN load me up in a bus and brought me to the airport. Some of my group mates were waiting at the airport to say goodbye before I left for America. Many other people from the camp were surrounding the airport that day to watch the plane took off.

When the plane took off, in my mind I wanted to look outside of the window of an airplane to see how its look like down on ground from above. However, it didn't go well than I imagined. Not even a minute after the plane take off that I felt noshes. I almost threw up so I put my head down between my knees and not look out of the window. Every time I wanted to lift head to look around, I got dizzy and nervous. Therefore, I kept my head down all the way to Kenyatta international airport in Nairobi.

"Be brave always in time of hardship in order to avoid being dishonored when the situation get better tomorrow or the next day."

CHAPTER 22

"The day I came to America."
Nairobi Kenya

It was morning time when I reached to Kenyatta international airport. I do not remember the exact time but I know it was morning because the sun was not too hot and my shadow was pointed north south position. The IOM agency person was already there waiting for me with a bus at the airport to brought me to where I was going to be waiting for my flight to come in the next five days. The police stopped our bus driver for the loud music as I was in bus heading to the compound where the IOM wanted me to stay while waiting for my flight date. It was a cassette of Mohammad Wardi's songs. Deng Matoto gave it to a bus driver so we all could listen to it. It was happy moment for me to be in different place other than Kakuma refugee camp. The police didn't give any ticket to a bus driver but just a warning and he told the driver to reduce the volume.

It was one big building with two floors and with only small rooms inside of it. My bed was very small but it was better than sleeping on floor without mattress. I had food three times a day, in morning, afternoon, and in the evening.

The UNHCR and IOM were renting this place for the refugees that being transfer to Nairobi hospital for better treatment, people who were in critical condition. And the people who were going to Canada and other places. There were some people already in that place so it was a little bite crowded. Therefore, bathroom was a big issued to everyone in that house. Water for showered, drinks, and foods were available except toilet. There were few of the toilets in the compound but not enough for everyone. In fact, these toilets were not working properly so to get rid of your waste then you had to put water in different separate bucket and pour them down into the toilet in order to flush. There was always long line every morning or any time of the day for the people wanted to use the bathroom. "You have to wait for your turn in order to use a toilet". "It wasn't good to waited on line to use a bathroom when you had diarrhea in that IOM facility". Even though there was more food to eat, I came up with my own idea not to eat too much so I don't have to use a toilet more often in a day. My body already got used to not having so much any way.

The bus driver came back the next day to bring me to the dentist, which was located on the other side of city. This was only part of medical fulfillment the IOM medical team didn't carry out in Kakuma. They for save it in order to do it in Nairobi. I had no idea where I was on that day. The dentist's office was very close to the highway. So while I was waiting for my turn to go in and see the doctor. I sat on bunches inside the fence at the dentist's office facing toward the highway.

I watched rush hour traffic going by, many cars fast every second. I tried to count every car going by but I lost count. Other thing distracted me such as airplane flew over head so low and with so much noise.

It was whole day process due to large number of people wanted to see the doctor on the same day. As the result, the UNHCR workers prepared breakfast and lunch for rest of the lost boys who were at the dentist's office and I. The bus driver didn't have time to bring people back to the compound for lunch. Due to rush hour, heavy traffic and long distance back to the compound made it impossible to go back and forth four ways a day.

I had already enough to eat when I came back from doctors' office to the compound where I was staying. There was food already waiting for me at the compound but I did not eat. I went to bed straight instead because I was also so exhausted. It was dark anyway and almost bed time when I got to the compound.

Perhaps going to the dentist's office the first day wasn't the last day ever than I thought it would be. I went back the next day not to see the doctor for my teeth clean but to help at the dentist's office. I put the chairs in places for patients to use in waiting room. From 5/10/2001 to 5/13/2001, I had been going to dentist's office to do my job. It was very fun job, because no much to it at all and everybody at the office were very nice to me. I charted most of the time with Kenyan workers at the dentist's office. My paycheck of thirty-shilling Kenyan helped me out at the Kenyatta international airport. I used it to buy myself some snack and hand sculpture of a giraffe to remind me of Africa.

On 5/14/2001 around 7:00 o-clock p.m, The IOM person in charge came in to make an announcement about the departure time in the morning. He said to me to get ready in the morning before 8:00 o-clock A.M for the bus driver to brought me to the airport for the 10:00 A.m. o-clock Am flight to Amsterdam.

I didn't sleep well that night after the announcement. I was anxious to be on airplane to America. Perhaps I was the first one up the next morning. I jumped in a shower got out, got dress and then putted my luggage together and waited for a bus driver to come. The bus driver beeps the horn when he entered the gate.

He was trying to warn everybody that he was arrived so people flying on that day could get ready and moved into a bus for drop off at the airport.

This time the bus driver took different rout through the city to the airport so I was able to see some of the tall buildings in Nairobi city. The rout that a bus driver took last time when he picked me up from the airport to the IOM's compound after my arrival from Kakuma refugee camp was a little bit longer and far away from the city. Therefore, I didn't see much of Nairobi city buildings.

The bus driver stopped at the drop off area at the airport. He got out of the car and shook my hands as I got out of the car in passenger side door. He said goodbye and good lucky my friends. The IOM person was already at the airport waiting for me to lead me where I need to be. The checked me in early so the IOM person could leave to go and take care of other lost boys in different airport.

I had two hours to kill before my flight departure time. I was able to explore inside the airport. I saw many amazing things such as Africa culture sculpture shops with so many hands made wood sculpture displayed every corner of the shop. In fact, I bought one of the Africa hand made sculpture wood giraffe to remind me of mother Africa.

I didn't have any suitcase just only the IOM plastic handbag was my carrier. I had few of my clothes together with my travel documents in that plastic bag. The flight attendant asked me if I had another bag so she could put away. I didn't even open my mouth to say no, I just lift up my IOM plastic had bagged to show it to her. She noted her head without saying anything at all she walked away. There were very good number of us without suitcases or regular bags but only plastic bag on that day in plane.

I was in center of the airplane so I didn't have chance to look out of the window. I was glad I sat in center anyway because I had the same fear of throwing up again like before from Kakuma refuge camp to Nairobi. In fact, I did the same thing I did when I was in airplane from Kakuma refugee camp to Nairobi, putting my head down between my knees. Since it was a long ride, I got over my fear later after couple of hours in air.

Another challenge I face in plane from Nairobi to Amsterdam was using a bathroom in plane for a first time ever it was not easy for me to use a bathroom in plane. I was afraid I would fall out of the plane. Getting up to walk to the bathroom makes me shaking. I tried to avoid going to the bathroom in a plane many time by holding it in as long as I could. The IOM trainee did a little bit demonstration how to use a restroom in a plane during orientation in Kakuma refugee camp, Kenya. "So I was totally did not know how to used a restroom the matter was that I was scared of height."

CHAPTER 23
Amsterdam

I did not know where I was when I got out of the plane in Amsterdam airport; it was dark. I could not see anything even a sign, I was sleepy. They must announce where we were landing while I was still sleeping. As got out of the gate the IOM person was standing there with the IOM sign in his hand. When I left Kakuma refugee camp they told me to look for IOM sign person in every airport I landed to and that what I did all the way until I reach to Vermont. I saw the IOM sign and I walked toward him. The rest of the lost boys did the same. We filed up in one single line and walked all the way to other side of airport terminal where they board me that day to New York. At the Amsterdam airport, when I look around all I see was people staring at me with wondering faces and questions in their minds. Where are these children going? Where they are coming from? They turn to one another and whisper with smile on their faces. I didn't know what they were saying. May be some thing means or they were feel sorry for me. Even the IOM agency person who was supposed to look after me insulted me just the moment I got out of the plane. I was smiling and he said, what happened to your teeth did you swallow them? Of course, some of my lower and upper teeth were missing because they never grew in. to his culture that was a joke but to my culture, it was definitely an insult to me. I was so angry. I open my mouth and close it back up almost says some thing bad to him. "I didn't want to get lost in different world where I don't know my way around." Though I swallowed my bad sentence, which I was going to say to him, instead I did say to him not to worry, I was not going to take his teeth. He looks at me and says nothing he didn't understand what I was saying. He was busy getting every other lost boy together out of plane so he didn't really ask me back what I was saying to him. Good thing he did not because I was not in mood to repeat myself.

At least not all of them where saying bad things about me on that day at the airport, may be half of them. However, most of them were nice and with sympathy inside them. I could tell the look on their face when I fast by carrying only just IOM plastic handbag in my hand. They wave at me with face of mercy and pity. I waved back at them too. I didn't have a chance to get close to those people and tell them not to worry I'm save now but to pray for rest of my friends who left behind so they could come to America.

The IOM person put me in a plane to New York the same day I was arrived to Amsterdam airport. I was so exhausted from long hours of plane ride from Jomokenyatta airport, Nairobi to Amsterdam. Those were total of nine hours in plane, sitting in one spot without stand up and walk around.

Before the plane took off, the flight attendant wheels her service table next to my seat and she asked me if I need tea or coffee. I said tea please I never had a coffee before so I don't know what that coffee going to do to me! I said, she smiles and she reached down under her service table to grab tea cup. She pours tea in a cup and then she handed to me. "She said be careful it's a little hot." She smiles and shakes her head and walk away to next person. It was around 7:00 Am so it was breakfast time. She was good looking girls, I was staring at her the whole time she was service me. May be that was one of the reason she told me to be careful with tea when she handed to me, because my eyes were all over her. That was one of the first rules of the welcome to the United States guidebook for Refugees I broke on that day in KLM plane. During orientation in Kakuma refugee camp, a person training me told me not to star at someone continuously. It is rude and it makes a person uncomfortable.

After I finished my tea and bagel then I fell back to sleep until the same flight attendant lady woke me up again for lunch. At first she asked me if I'm a vegetarian or not. I told her that I can eat any thing. She didn't ask me what I want it though. "She just started put everything on my lunch table including salad and I never had salad before!" of course I didn't tell her to stop putting all these food on my lunch table because I wanted to eat. "One of my friend who was sitting next to me said I'm not a cow I'm not eating salad." only cow eat uncooked green leaves. I ate some of my salad though I didn't finish it all; I eat half of it. I told my friend to tried it and he said no way I'm not touching that salad! My friend was skeptical about salad because it was new thing to him and me as well.

I was in center of the plane the whole time from Nairobi to Amsterdam and from Amsterdam to New York so I didn't get a chance to look out at the window. It was night time too in most of the ride.

CHAPTER 24
New York

When I was arriving to JFK airport in New York city on may 16/2001, it was night and my flight to Burlington Vermont was schedule for next day in the morning.

The IOM case worker in New York took me and other lost boys to a hotel lodge to spend night and then leave in the morning. He told me to set my alarm clock for six oclocks AM to get ready to head to the airport at eight o-clock flight to Burlington.

There were alarm clocks in very room. I was so exhausted, I went to bed right away as soon as I check in. I didn't even think of eating that night or set my alarm clock for that matter until the next morning. There were all kind of food in my room; bagel, banana, and apple on table, milk and juices in bridge. I did wake up early that day though and help myself with food before the IOM case worker showed up to transport me to the airport. In fact I slept so well that night on mattress. It was my first time ever to sleep on nice comfortable mattress bed. I thought I was going to leave right away to Vermont when I arrived to the airport that day. My imagination was miscalculated. I waited for my flight to Vermont for whole day until three oclocks in the afternoon. I didn't have any money to buy something eat or drink.

The only thing available in the airport waiting area which I didn't want money to buy it was water. It wasn't until around 5 PM when they finally board me into a plane to Burlington Vermont. It was small plane so I was able to see out side through the window because I was sitting by the window. It started to get dark before I even take off. This time I never fall a sleep from New York to Vermont. I was awake all the way to Burlington. I saw very interesting views while in air. So many different colors of lights appeared from down below. Some of these color lights were red, yellow, flashing yellow or red, blue light, and whole range of flashing bright lights. I turn to a person sitting next to me and I asked him about all these kinds of lights down there. He looks at me with surprise face! It took him couple second to respond to my idiot question. He didn't say a word the whole time. He thought I was joking but he saw my IOM plastic hand bag between my seats. He knew where I come from and he figured out that I'm new to the area and everything is new to me as well. So he started to explain to me the purpose of flashing lights. He said the red, green; yellow are traffic lights on the street.

People set the lights that way at night to flash when there is no heavy traffic, he said. Then he continued with more explanation about the purposes of blue light.

The blue light you see down there are in runway. It shows the pilot where to land a plan. I was staring at him the whole he explains. Then after he finished answering my questions, I said to him thank you. I didn't ask him what his name was though. But after I said thank you to him, he asked me what my name was?

Then I said Peter Abui. John he said. I do not remember his last name just only his first name John. I still remember his first name because it's a common name where I come from. There were so many John in my group in Kakuma camp. So it was easy for me to remember his first name than his American name. The conversation kept on going, John asked me where I was coming from. I was going to answer his question but unfortunate the plane land and we all went in separate ways.

CHAPTER 25
Burlington Vermont

When I walked out of the gate through the exit door, I was looking for an IOM person with an IOM sign. It turns out no more IOM agent in Burlington Vermont airport to direct me where I need to go. They were people from Episcopal Church and one caseworker from Vermont refugee resettlement program were waiting for me at the Burlington airport on that day of my arrival to Vermont. Everybody rush to me with arms spread out to hug me when I was walking out of the plane through the terminal. They did not even have my name on post sign to holding up on their hands for me to see. I was surprised how they know me. Then I realize that they know me because of the IOM plastic handbag I was carrying. I remember Joyce coral was there on the night of 5/17/2001 when I came to State of Vermont. It turns out this was the day I got marriage eight years later. I did not even know I would get marriage on the day I came to my new home, America. For me it is double celebration I should do every this time of the year.

Entering to State of Vermont was the happiest day of my life. From that day, I knew I was in right place. Seeing all the people which I didn't even met before in my life; came rushing to me with their arms spread out wanted to give me hugs and the posts with word welcomes to Vermont written all over the posting paper that they were holding up made me shed tears of joy.

I felt the care and love that day at the Burlington airport from friends from all the churches here in State of Vermont and the people of Vermont, including Vermont refugee resettlement program.

I remembered when caseworker from Vermont refugee resettlement program took me to my hosting family in Winooski. A caseworker did not tell me who was going to stay with me until I stepped to that door. It was Atem Deng who opened the door that day and his roommates were there too. Deng Ayach,

Panther Ayuen, Atem Deng, Dau, and Chol Kiir Atem were my South Sudanese hosting family in 2001 when I came to States of Vermont. This family was one group of the lost boys from South Sudan who came to Vermont from Kakuma refugee camp before me. I knew them when I was in

Kakuma. They were my friends and group neighbors. We used to go to church together. These people showed me around Vermont especially the refugee resettlement program's office to get some clothes and other things that I needed. Vermont refugee resettlement program was the only place I wanted to be in first seven weeks of my arrival to Vermont. I needed to be situated by the people of Vermont refugee resettlement program first before I go anywhere far.

My hosting family had been in Vermont too long so they know their ways around to every locations. They had American family friends so every weekend they took me there to play soccer and back yard picnic. Their friend became my friend too.

After one month later, my caseworker found an apartment for five other lost boys and I in Colchester Vermont to rented. Simon Gai, Abraham Malual, Denyjok Aguot, Benjamin Achiek Machar, and Peter Abolish Keny were my roommates.

The house rent was $1200 plus utilities. Between six of us it was not so bad even though I did not have a job yet. Each of us pay $200 plus utilities. My only in come was food stamp and $ 500 from Vermont refugee resettlement program a month. I did not want to live on food stamp so long; I wanted to find a job soon so I could get my own money. However, it was up to caseworker to hook me up with a job. At least that what they told me during orientation in Kakuma refugee camp that it's responsibility of the refugee resettlement agency of the state you had been selected to hosting you to find the first job for me. My first job was janitor at UVM. It was summer however; I spend most of the time outside cleaning the windows in buildings all round the campus. It was fun. I was very happy I got the job where I could earn my own money. The distant to my job was quiet far away. In addition, with only bike as my main transportation, it was hard for me to get to work on time. I had to wake early morning so I could get to work on time. Some time I walked instead of riding my bike to work. One day I was on my way to work ride the bike in the morning the Burlington police pull me over for riding my bike on main road and not on bike path. The police told me that it is too dangerous to rid bike on road without a bike lane. The North AVE road got bike path but it is a little out my way.

Therefore, the only short cut was route six through Burlington and straight to UVM. From that, I started walking to work by foot. Some time I Called mama Jean or George Cross to give me a ride to work.

My caseworker found me another job at Birchwood Nursing home as a house Keeping before winter arrived. This job was four miles away from my house that make it a lot easy for me to get to work on time. Everybody was nice to me at work. I did house keeping job for three months time and then they change my shift to 3rd Shift so I could do laundry. That's was fun job ever. Every night I was the only one in laundry mate. Therefore, that made my job even more fun. When felt lonely or bored in a laundry mate, I always turned the radio on, not loud and I started dancing while folding clothes at the same time. The nurse heard the music so they came in tiptoeing to watch me dancing. I had to go round 6th times to picked up dirty clothes in patients' rooms and in a hallway so I can wash them.

Every time I fast by the nurses' station, the nurses smiling at me. I did not know why? Until one day, I caught them standing at the door watching me danced then I realized this is the reason the nurses smile at me every time I fast by at the nurses' station.

After couple of years working in Nursing home, I decided to changed my job status and become patients support as a starting point forward. Since I came to America from Africa, I wanted to do electrical. However, I did not want to start with electrical job right away. I wanted to get familiar with the environment on job. However, I started with non-construction job, get closer with people, and learn communication skill. Therefore, I applied at Fletcher Allen health care. This time there was no help from caseworker from refugee office, I did it on my own.

Getting a job at Fletcher Allen health care did work out well because some of my roommates were working at Fletcher Allen health care at the time. Therefore, we were carpooling together some time when we were working on the same shift.

My doctor's office was close to Fletcher Allen hospital. It was easy to make my appointment there and go back to work after the appointment. "There are always bumps on job but I didn't let those pull me backward." I just want go forward doing my job right. I was doing same job I was doing at Birchwood trace as a house keeping before I became a laundry man. Working at Fletcher Allen health care was great. Job was fun and people were friendly. In fact, I made many friends there in a hospital.

The Vermont refugee resettlement program hired a tutor to give me head start on school. This class was all English basic, which was English as a second language. I even took a trip to ST. Michael's college for TOFEL class. I wanted to determine where to start my school. I wanted to either go to high school or go to CCV College. At first, I wanted to take classes at CCV but after English as a second language test at the end made people of refugee office decided to let me go to high school. It was not easy with State of Vermont school board for me to go to high school because of my age. However, the State school board understood my background situations therefore, they compromise to let me joint high school.

After all, state of Vermont is the only state allowed lost boys of south Sudan to joint high school. Even some of my from other states came to Vermont so they can go to high school.

At the time, I was going to school full time and working full time. I go to school in the morning from 7: AM to 2:30 PM in the afternoon then went straight to work after school. I started work at 3:00 PM to 11:30 PM everyday five days a week.

Some time I do not get home until 1:00 in morning because of transportation issue. Once I got home then I tried to do my homework which would take me one hour to hour and half to complete my homework, that's give me six hours to sleep before I got up for school on next day. I walked home some time if I do not have any money for Yellow cab. I do not call someone for ride in middle of night however; the only option is to walk home. After I started school, my schedule changed to 3rd shift so I can go to school in the morning. I used to carpool with some my friends but once I started school, their shift did not change as my, they were still working in the morning.

I was so happy to get my first car and my own driving license. It did not take me too long to drive my own car in the first time after my face image was on driving license; I could not wait. George Cross helped Peter Keny, Denyjok Aguot, and I to find our own car.

One day I was driving to school and there was a person head of me driving truck with a boat hooked on a trailer. I did not really know what has had happened on that day. In a blink of an eye, I was right there on his tailgate. I tried to slam on a brake but it was too late to proven the accident; Therefore, I hit the boat engine in front of me. The good thing I had car insurance with progressive at that time.

Even though my car was not taking care of because it on liability, it was nice, the insurance fixes the boat, otherwise I would have paid it out of my own pocket. I did not have that kind of money to fix the boat. Mrs. Pam Landry came to cheer me up during the accident. She helped me contact my insurance agent that day.

Since I moved to my new place in Colchester Vermont, I was not comfortable.

One of my neighbors made it so hard for me to live there. She did not like me living next to her in that apartment for some reasons. She mad fails phone calls to my property owner every single day complaining about not truce staffs.

Therefore, I had to explain myself to my landlord every single phone call she made. I guess for me leaving the lights on for too long in my house or parking my car in a circle or along side the road or turned my car light on direct to her house was the problem. I tried to stay out of her sight in order to avoid more fails phone calls from her to my property owner. My other neighbors had no any problem at all whatsoever.

It even became worse, when one of my roommates drove the car through into one of the neighbors' house.

I could not handle it any more so I decided to move away to different place. I looked around for some apartment to rent and I found one in Essex junction Vermont. Peter Keny, Daniel Gai Ayuom and I moved in together to one house in town of Essex junction. In my new place, I never see any sign of rejecting on my new neighbors faces. In fact, I do not get to see them that more often during the day or night. I got up so early in the morning to go to school while my neighbors were still sleeping. Moreover, I got home every night late from work while the neighbors were already in bed.

I did not have many friends in high school because kids were all under age. I tried to stay away as I could. The kids were nice to me and they wanted to become my friend. I acted as an adult so they were respecting my boundaries that I set for myself. I had no time after school anyway to hang around. Teachers were nice to me too. They knew my situations so they were okay with me being quiet in class and hand it in my work late sometime. Lauren Kirby couillard was there in Essex high school as assistant principal. She might tell all the teachers about me that I am one of the lost boys of South Sudan who just came to the State from Kakuma refugee camp. She was my first turning point teacher at Colchester high school. I was having hard time understand American accents at school and even at work. I was just very much Reading books and do my homework base on a book I read.

My first year in high school was very much struggling. I was having hard time with American history, English, and math. I remember writing my life story for project in Colchester high school. The only word pop up out of my mind on that day was I see a "loin". However, I wrote down on my paper I see a loin that is it. That was supposed to be the topic but I could not think more for some reason. I handed it in just that sentence to my teacher Mrs. Lauren. She did not ask me to continue with the story. I think she understood my frustration on first day in school.

In PE/gym class, the teachers expect me to do everything just like other American kids in class. I never do roller skate or ski ever before in my life. I tried anyway for the sake of my grades even though I did not do well in any of them. I had fun though doing ski but not roller-skating. I just picked up my roller skating and walked along with class to where we were going. The children were laughing at me but I didn't care at all. During snowboarding period, not a single time I went straight without falling down. Good thing it was snow not a dry land, it was not hurt falling down on snow and that why I kept doing it otherwise I would just picked up my snowboard and walk away. It was cold though but I was not allowed to go back inside by myself without the whole class.

The teachers were working together helping me toward fulfilled my education goal. They invited the people from technical college to came to Colchester high to tell me more about course and majors I should considered when I decided to go to college after I graduated from high school. I didn't tell any teacher in Colchester high school what I want to be, I was freshman and I didn't have a guidance councillor by then. May be I did have a guidance canceller but I don't remember going to his/her office.

In my high school year, most of the times I just want to work alone on every school project. Seem like I think a lot better every time when I was working a lone in class. Kids some time were ignorance since English is my second language, they had hard time understand my accent and I don't understand what they were saying either. When I explain something orally, they don't get it unless I wrote it down on paper. "They looked at me with wondering faces!"

"I don't remember how many times they ask me where I'm from?" they notice that I was not from here. The site in-group before the teacher arrived talking and peek at me while I was reading in corner of the class. I can tell they were talking about me but I did not care because they were younger than I was. Beside, none of them said something offense in my face. I was a little shy at the time therefore, my participation grades in class was very low. Raising my hand to answer any questions was limited. I did it couple time but with my accent and poor English speaking, they laugh at me. Perhaps, I decided to just listen, do my work and not raise my hand to answer any question unless the teacher picks me to answer certain question on that class period.

In Essex high school a woman from VSC came to school for college financial aid application process. I wanted to go to Casselton state college I even submitted my application to that college. Unfortunate that did not happen, not because they rejected me. It was change of a plan that I made after I talked with my guidance cellar. When I told her I want to be electrician, she advised me to just joint Vermont electrical apprentice program. She connected me with Karen Archer from Essex tech and Karen talked to me more about the program. Karen and Lauren invited electrical inspector Mr. Dennis J. Downer for details regard apprenticeship program. Mr. Dennis was teaching electrical apprentice class at Vermont technical college at the time and he became my four-year electrical apprentice teacher.

A month before my graduation, I applied to Union training center for an electrical job and they accepted me. Of course, Mrs. Lauren Couillard wrote a recommendation for me to send to any college I wanted to apply. I did sent this recommendation letter together with my college application to Castellon State College and to Union training center as well. Below is the letter of recommendation that Mrs. Lauren Couillard wrote on September 15, 2004

> September 15, 2004
>
> To whom it may concern:
>
> I am pleased to recommend Peter Abui for admission to any college of his choice. I have known Peter for over three years, and observed him display not only competent language and writing skills, but positive leadership skills as well.
>
> I first met Peter when he was a student in my ninth grade humanities course at Colchester High School during the academic year, 2001-2002. Peter struggled with English (both written and oral articulation) but he worked extremely hard to succeed. Although he had taken English classes at the Refugee camp in Kenya, it was clear that Peter needed further instruction in his written and oral expression.

The ninth grade humanities course included both reading of several novels including Night, he Odyssey, The Red Scarf Girl, Nectar in A Sieve, and many independent reading books. There was also much analytical writing involved in the understanding of these novels. Peter is conscientious, very aware of his academic performance, and works diligently to improve on his written and oral and articulation skills. In addition, Peter takes initiative with written projects and essays and often meets or exceeds standard on completion. He is not afraid to work and with revising and editing his work. Peter is and independent learner and he work best when given some direction, but is give enough breathing room to complete tasks with his own personal flair. I have no doubt that Peter will take his academic studies seriously and will succeed at whatever major he chooses.

I have personally known Peter for the entire time that he has been in the United States. I know him to be extremely responsible, a hard worker, and a good friend. His introduction to the culture of the United States was difficult, and Peter always took every situation as a challenge to overcome. He moved to Essex Junction in 2003-2004 and I have had the pleasure of keeping in touch with him. He has also spoken about his difficult journey through Africa in my English classes during the time he has been a student in Essex. This was amazing information for the students, and an excellent public speaking experience for Peter.

I have every confidence that he will be successful in post high school pursuits. Please give Peter consideration for admission to your institution. If you have any questions bout Peter Majuch Abui or this recommendation, please contact me at this number?

Sincerely,

Lauren Couillard

Assistant Principal
(Former English Teacher)

I was going to start working at union right away after I graduated from high school but I found a job at Omega electric company before I graduate. They wanted me to start as soon as possible. Therefore, I went and work for Omega electric company instead. I started working there on 6/21/2005 that was after my high school graduation though. Karen made working for Omega electric company possible. She introduced me to one of Omega's project manager Mr. Steve Baker.

She even gave me Omega electric office phone number to call. However, I decided to just go in myself and feel out an application instead of making phone call. I afraid no one would understand me on phone. I always afraid of that mater of English accent that no one will hear me clearly on phone. I was very happy to start my career at Omega electric thanks to Mr. Al Senecal for welcome me to his company. I am always proud of working at Omega electric company. My bosses and co-workers are very friendly since the day I started working for Omega electric company until today date. Two of my co-workers were the first people I worked with in Winooski Vermont garage on very first day in 2005. They shown me every thing I want to know and do on my first day on job site. I was lost not know what to do but they didn't let me wondering around on job site on my own.

Perhaps, not every person was nice to me on my first day and along the years I been in trade for that mater. I remember my first day on job site as an electrician apprentice; it was not fun at all. I don't even know how many times I stepped up and down on that ladder. I did a lot of running up and down on those stairs all over the new construction building gathering electrical materials. I was very exhausted that day. I realized that construction job is not the same as the other normal regular job I did before. But that didn't stopped me from follow my dream of become electrician. I was blame many times, for what I did not do. No one believed me even though I told them I didn't do it. And the only thing they say back to me was "you are the only one new here." I tried very hard to control myself and not to put anyone or myself in trouble. "Instead, I deal with any blowing flame on my own way." "I considered everybody as my friend and that was my grip and I stick with it." "They undermine my expectation of performing on job because they assume I don't know much." then when I prove to them then the only thing they say to me is "you are smarter than you look." I did not care how many times I trip I never thing of going backward or any other direction. I got up and kept moving forward after my wishing dream to grabs.

At the end of the ship we all smile and happy. I was learning how not to take any thing personal. Since I never had a job before where I can interact with other coworkers,

I was sensitive to whatever people are saying behind my back.

Then after long years working with Americans friends I became familiar with systems that bosses sometime got harder on you in order to focuses on whatever you are sign to do.

I observe over the years and I learned that company is like a family. I experience it during Christmas parties and other company's gathering activities I had been to. People come together and celebrate; hug one another, laugh, and have fun.

I love Omega electric company Christmas party time. I always had a great time and I had to see people from the office and some of my co-workers who I didn't see for such a long time because of the different jobs sit we all working on.

Thank to Al Senecal and Cheryl Senecal for making Christmas party happen every year.

I was still going to high school at the time and she was in culinary institute college in Essex Junction Vermont. We met through a friend who used to be her friend at first. She went to Nantucket for internship before she graduated. She graduated from college in October/2005 after I graduated from high school. On that day, she moved to Nantucket I went with her to help her moved. I remember calling out from school because I was in Winchendon Massachusetts on my way to Nantucket. We spent night at her aunt Audrey Christian's house and we moved on the next morning to Nantucket. That was the first time I met her aunt Audrey's family. Uncle Mark, Alli Christian, Jessica Basso, and Tyler were there on that day of my pasting through. We drove four hours from Winchendon Massachusetts to Hyannis to take a ferry to Nantucket, which took us another two, and half hours to Nantucket Island. We got to Nantucket before dark. Pat check in to her apartment where she was going to stay. The manger of the reassurance where Patricia was going to be working invited Pat and I and plus other three people who were there for an internship as well, for especial welcome dinner. It was also a welcoming dinner and a task out whatever on menu.

That was the first time ever I ate snail accidentally. It was taste good though. The snail dish was under different name Escargot on seafood section menu. I did not know it was a snail and I did not ask the waiter for that mater. If I knew, it was a snail I would have eat it anyway because Escargot was delicious. 21 federal reassurances was the name of the reassurance. Patricia explain it to me afterward what was it after we went back to apartment.

I spent two days in Nantucket, Saturday and Sunday. I came back to Vermont on Monday morning so I could go to School otherwise I would just stay there with my girlfriend. I had to go back to Nantucket every other weekend to see her. One day Patricia called to warn me not to come because of the storm but I came anyway to surprise her. She told me to find an apartment so we both can move in together when she comes back from Nantucket. I started looking around for an apartment and I found one bedroom apartment in Williston Vermont. I moved in first in August/2005 while she was still in Nantucket. She came back from Nantucket to Vermont on Labor Day of 2005. She had to go back to Nantucket that weekend to help in reassurance. We live in Williston apartment for ten months then we moved to Varennes Vermont on 6/21/2006 to a bigger apartment. Two weeks before she moved back to Vermont, I went back to Nantucket and propose to her to marriage me. I knew the day I saw her she was the one so I decided to not this opportunity dissolve in my eyes. She loves me just who I am; she did not care where I was coming from or how poor I was. She cares so much about me. My family already accepted her even though they did not meet her yet. 5/17/2008 was the day I started my new life in America. We got marriage on the day above in St. Andrew church, Essex Vermont. This day is the pine point of my history. 5/17/2001 was the day I came to America and 5/17/2008 was the day got marriage; I should be celebrating this day twice.

We went through so much pain together since the day we met. She had miscarriage before we got engage. It was tough time but we got through it together as one. After miscarriage, it was Hodgkin Lymphoma cancer. Two weeks later after she found out she was pregnant; she was diagnoses with stage three Hodgkin lymphoma cancers. In the beginning the Dr. did all kind of test on Patricia in order to determine what type of cancer it was and what stage the cancer reached. Of course, they did X-ray first follow by surgery for laminose test.

Then along the way more tests followed, patscan, bonemero, and MRI. The Dr. was concern about giving her chemotherapy while she was pregnant and so do we. The Dr. wanted to wait until the baby was born to start a chemo. At first, she wanted to terminate the baby in order to start chemo treatment. However, cancer was in advance stage three already and the baby was grown big to a stage where it was not possible to do abortion. That was even more high risk to wait that long to start chemo or to take the baby out of her. The only option left was to go a head with chemo treatment and hope for the best. The Dr. wanted to wait until first trimester of pregnancy to give green light for chemo treatment. In fact, Patricia wanted to keep the baby because this baby means a lot to her. In addition, for me at that moment it was a mater of saving two lives otherwise I would just purpose abortion option in order to do chemo treatment right away to save one live. "It was hard time for both of us to make a wise decision on something like that!" The Dr. was supportive and caring about our situation. She even did some research on one woman who had been in the same problem as Patricia. The Dr. gave us the phone number of that woman so we could talk to her and ask some questions to learn more about the out come of having chemo while pregnant. I belief Patricia call her and talk to her I did not get the information about that phone call because I was at work on that day. "Whatever they tell themselves that day I do not know."

Now the first trimester was past, total maximum of fifteen weeks. The Dr. is ready to start chemo treatment on Patricia as scheduled. On 3/17/2006 was the day she received the chemo treatment. Perhaps, going to Doctor's office was regularly bases visited. I was the only one working at the time but we were doing well in term of money wise. She was on Medicaid insurance. However, on medical part, it was not an issue at all. Nevertheless, the whole situation was eating us a life from inside. I go to work every morning and getting out from work early some time so I could take my wife to Doctors for her appointment was challenging. I missed most of time from work and my boss was okay with it; he was understandable of my situation. I remember driving her to hospital in middle of night couple of times. 7/15/2006 was the night I brought her to Fletcher Allen health care hospital because she was experiencing contractions. We spent that night in hospital until the next day when the baby was born. With chemo and pregnancy, she was sick most of the time. She was hard time breathing couple of times and diarrhea on top of it. Of course, her feet were swelling as well and nausea was obvious. She was on her 6 cycle of chemo treatment when she had the baby. She never stops taking chemo from the day she started until the day the baby was born. Indeed her pregnancy was at high risk so every doctor that was involve in her treatment were all alert to come to delivery room; the chemo Doctor, critical team, and OB Doctor Blake were all there in labor and delivery room. The room was full of doctors and nurses. The doctors let her grandmother Benet stays with her so to hold her hand during pushing time. I myself and other family members were outside in waiting room. Proverbially she did more name calling at the time of pushing but I was not there in room grandmother Benet was the one her hands got squeeze hard.

It went well that night; there was no complication through out the process of delivering the baby. After the baby arrived the nurse run out into waiting room to grab me so I could cut umbilical cord but I told doctor to just go a head and cut the umbilical cord.

God almighty was watching over us all this times. He heard our voice calling him for his blessing. However, he was listing after all. In fact, I never stop calling God to look over me since the day I left South Sudan and to all the refugee camps, I had been to. My first son Maluchy Michael Abui was born on 7/16/2006 as one healthy boy. Even though he came two moths early than his due date, because of what his mother was going through, sickness, he was strong and health. Of course, he could not come home right away in couple of days after he was born because of the whole situation. Therefore, he had to spend three weeks in Nicu at Fletcher Allen health care hospital to recover little bit before he comes home.

He could not suck on baby's bottle on his own yet. The nurses used feeding tub to put the food in his stomach. My sons was 4Ib ½ onuses when he was born. We had to stay at Ronald McDonald's house for those three weeks in order to be close to him. I had to go to work in morning and my wife Patricia had to go to the hospital to stay with our son.

The day he came home and the day he was born was the most joyful days of our life. He was so tiny I always afraid I will drop him when I holding him on my arms.

The nurse told me to hold him against my chest so he could feel skin-to-skin contact, is good for him. Every time I go to nick, I pick him up and put him on my chest then rock him. He could not open his little tiny eyes so I sat on rocking chair and then rock back and forth very slowly. I wanted him to open his eyes so while I was rocking him, I said, opened your eyes buddy daddy and mommy are here. He just blinked very quickly and went back to sleep.

I remember the first day of his coming home from a hospital; I was so excited to see my little boy coming home. We put his crib beside our bed. He did well on his first day at home. He woke up a couple of times at night but after we changed his diaper and feed him he always went back to bed for a couple of hours. I remember giving him his first bath, he loves water but he does not like water in his face. Because of what we were going through, I did not have time to attend parent-training class. Therefore I learn how to changed baby's diaper on TV. I was ready to become a father every since the day we found out we are going to be parents. Perhaps, his mother watched over him first before me because the baby was in her belly. I did my part too as parent before the baby was born. I was sending to get Chinese food in middle of night couple of times. Of course,

Chinese reassurance was close at night so I could not get the Chinese food until next morning.

The chemo continues flowing into her body in big amount after the baby was born. She thought her going to lose her hair because of the chemotherapy so she shaved her head. She went and get wig to wear; unfortunately, she did not lost her hair a cording to her expectation.

The miracle happened; the Dr. told her that on the last test that she was on mission from cancer. She had to go back every five years for check up to make sure the cancer is not coming back.

Three years latter after my son Maluchy Was born, we had another child,

Methderow Ashton Abui. He was born on 11/09/2009. Then Methderow, Majuch Kenneth Abui was born four years latter. It had been blessing moment of our life.

Having my wife Patricia Abui beside our three beautiful children and me was everything I ever wanted. Now my older boy is in third grade and the second one is in preschool. I always happy and proud every time of my boys' work at school. I read couple of my son Maluchy papers that he wrote for class project. He wrote what he was thankful for during Thanksgivings time.

"Here what he wrote: I am thankful for food because I would starve to death."

I had been telling them a bout my pass life that I did not have enough food to eat for long time. I told them to be thankful every time for whatever they have in their lives, family as one of them.

I remember my first time going to parent teacher conferences as a father, I was so very proud and happy of my son's work in school.

I always wanted to have my own place for my family since I came to United States of America. Getting my own place was one of my dreams goals I always wish to accomplish. However, of course, in my mind education was always the first priority when I came to America. Follow by having a family, then settle down in normal life, and tried to blend in with American communities. My wife Patricia and I decided to buy a house so we could live in all together. We knew that we are going to have more than one child and an apartment in Vergennes we were living in was very small for the family. Therefore, we went and bought a house in Swanton Vermont. We both established our credit good at the time however our credit scores were high. We let my father in-law come and live with us in Swanton. That was the best decision we ever made. He was so close to his grandchildren. He spends many times playing with his grandchildren; they were best friends. The children miss him so much after he died, especially Methderow my middle child. My third child Majuch Kenneth was not born yet back then. Now Methderow is so attaches to one of his grandfather's pillow. He loves that pillow so much he would not let go of it or use another pillow at all.

I did not want to have a family and be unable to give the support they need. I did not have many good things in my past life as a child. I did not want my children to face what I went through during all my childhood time of not having good food to eat, education, and a Doctor. I never have my own Doctor for that matter or went to a Doctor's office for regularly check up until the time I went for medical exam at IOM clinic center in Kakuma refugee camp, Kenya to come to America. I did not have my own bed or watch cartoons on TV. I never received gifts during Christmas time or on my birthday. I never celebrated any my birthdays so I did not really care or worry about the gifts anyway. In fact, I never did or have a lot good or fun stuffs in my life.

None of my parents were there to put me to bed at night and give me kisses. I was a lone taking care of myself, which mean I make my own decisions.

"For whatever happened to me all these years of my traveling all over the world looking for safety, make me so sensitive and always very protective over my children because I am afraid of what I had been through will never face them again."

"Hope is a powerful element of strength. Hope tomorrow will be better or the next day and never get discourage when it turn out to be worse day. Many tries might make a different than just giving it up."

"I thought I will never hear the word conflict or war again in South Sudan after the CPA agreement was sign with North Regime in 2005." I thought that was the moment we all the southernness had been waiting for all these years? I guess I was wrong after all, I underestimate the will of our leaders toward the country and the people.

On Sunday December 15 /2013 around 6:00 pm, I was on my face book page checking in as usual what every body being common on or post. As I, score down couple more posts while reading along at the same time. I came across to the news on Aljazeera English face book page about heavy shooting in Juba capital city of Southern Sudan. When I saw this post I didn't common anything on the page or ask what's going on in Juba because I thought it was some other small problem that always happening between two people. However, I worried though therefore, I bought a phone card to call my brother Maluch and some of my relatives who are living there in Juba, Southern Sudan in order to make sure they are okay. I always do call to Juba when I heard bad breaking news in Southern Sudan or in my village of Kalthok. I spend all Sunday night calling but phone did not get through at all; I went to bed. Next Monday morning I went to work at Fletcher Allen health care and work until 9:00 a.m. then I took a break. However, instead of eating my egg and hams breakfast, I made a phone call to my cousin Thon Abui; he answered his cell phone after three times ringing. I said Hello cousin Thon and he said hello back to me. I ask him how he is doing? Moreover, he said I am okay, he said and everybody else except your brother Maluch's wife Regina Ponie Kenny. She is dead the tank run her over last night while she was sleeping inside the hut with three of your nieces, a four month old baby name Mary Nyanlat, three-year-old Amath, and seven-yearold Ayen. When he said that line of death, I did not say anything for couple of minutes; my mouth was dry shot and the tears just drip down out of my eyes in less of second when I heard the bad news. He said hello are you there Majuch Gongich? I said yes I am here Thon; he thought the line was lost or something. He told me to stay strong, I said, nothing we can do what happen is happen, and it is all on our government. He said, at right now what we can do is to find the good care for this four month old baby Mary Nyanlat who had been left behind by her mother while she was breast feeding. My brother Maluch was in kalthok when incident happened otherwise he could be dead too. Therefore, after the attempt coup in Juba as they said it, everything was close down, no movement, people are telling to stay in theirs houses. Until then I have been calling to Kalthok and juba but the network was not cooperating at all. After the incident baby was not doing well, I got the phone called from my cousin Thon that Mary Nyanlat has been sick nonstop since the first day her mother died. I paid some money for doctor visited to be look at by doctors Thon said. When I heard the news, It makes me worry so much about her situation for just being a baby and she was depending on her mother breast milk. How she going to be able to survive without a proper hospital to provide her with nutrition she needs. How she going to make it through without her mother' hands touch and not to mention the conflict has spread out over the country of South Sudan therefore, no movement.

There was no good health care and a baby food that will take care of the conditions like Mary. My brother is already dying from inside about the whole situation; four baby girls without a mother and without a job or a help from government is tough for him to handle. The house was destroyed therefore, no place to live. I was supporting them by sending some money to buy food every other month but now they are going to expect more money from me because I am the only one here In the United States of America who have a job. My wife and I tried to bring the baby here to United States of America so she could recover from that whole situation. Unfortunately, we were denied by US immigration office. They told me that I cannot bring any of my extend family to America.

Even until then I still do not know what exact the cause of recently war that occurred on December of 2013 in Juba, South Sudan between the Government and the rebel group. Many lives of the South Sudanese people were lost on this war again! They were not supposed to go just like that without the taste of freedom. Of course, many of my family members were kills on that day. That was 2 years and 5 months after referendum for South Sudan to become independent country out of North regime Government. My fellow South suddenness people said things that they are not supposed to say toward this war in South Sudan.

However, I decided not to belief what everyone was telling me on a phone and on internet about the coursed of this war in South Sudan. Therefore, I stayed away from social network media such as a face book and others news media web sits. Because I was not agreeing, with whatever they were saying in public social media. I just wish for peace to come to South Sudan so the people can live in peace as one unifies country once for all.

ABOUT THE BOOK

"My life was full of many unexpected experiences." Some were good and some were bad.

"During that time of war mostly, bad times occurred more often than good times in my lifetime."

"Those good times didn't last longer."

"I think there is a reason why things happen to people and as always there are results afterward either good or bad."

My hope all along all the years of war in South Sudan was that, I always wish that one day there would be a joyful moment to me as the outcome of my horrible suffering. I do not have many good times to remember in my past life since the day I left South Sudan; I until the day I came to United States of America. However, even then still, I always feel like I'm missing something. Of course indeed, part of me is missing: My whole family is not here with me.

"I never give up on myself when I was in that horrible situation. I resisted the pain I was facing. I wish of no ravage that I should do against my foes for what they did to me. Instead, I wish to preach the word of peace to my enemy for the sack of freedom in order to save lives of innocent.

I wish to just Speak out only the word of Unify".

"I wanted to make the world aware of the war situation that was going on in my hometown and tried to convey only peace among the people and avoid more lives lost.

"War is wrong; we are all human being with only one common goal:" "Soul."

However, the only message you should be saying to your enemies is peace.

Bear in mind that when you are torturing someone, you are torturing yourself as well. "You might not feel it physically but emotionally may be not at the moment but afterward in the near future when peace comes and when the justice prevails." pubjpg